WEIGHTLESS

by Robert Rahula

ALSO BY ROBERT RAHULA

NOVELS:
Messieurs
Panamaniac
Island of Misfits
Day Another Paradise In
One Last Fling
Bathhouse Stories
Conversation in a Belgian Bar
All the Yage in Reno
Exigent Circumstances
Uninvited Guest
A Modest Summation of Things
To Die in Toledo
The Treasure of the Gran Ventura
Inauthenticity

SHORT STORIES:
Horror Stories for Children
Behind the Pearly Gates

POETRY:
Trigger Points
Dentro Del Corazón Bloqueada
Camino
Migration
I Sing the Body Politic
Wonderland
From Whose Bourn
Poemas Españoles
Expat Poems
Old Dogs New Poems

ANTHOLOGIES:
Half Life
The Essential Dan Landes
50 Years Down the Drain

Alma-gator Press
Barcelona • Madrid • La Chorrera

PROLOGUE

James Crown was looking for the perfect tropical paradise in which to set up shop. And he found it in the country of Panama—that small isthmus of land that connects Colombia to Central America. Panama had a history of welcoming US investors with open arms—open arms and eyes averted. Truth be told, Panama's economy is based on the trifecta of tourism, money laundering, and illicit businesses. In order for that kind of economy to function, the Panamanian government *had* to look the other way when it came to questions about the source or use of foreign investments. So, it was natural that when James Crown and his team of investors flew into Panama City, he was given the royal treatment by government officials. And when he explained to them his plan for opening a special resort for medical tourism in Panama, they knew of just the place. Government limousines whisked him to La Chorrera, a small city just forty minutes southwest of Panama City. La Chorrera was a tranquil mini-metropolis, nestled in the hills overlooking the calm Pacific waters of the Bay of Chance and the idyllic beach known as Playa Grande. La Chorrera was big enough to have most of the modern conveniences that an influx of rich tourists might want, but small enough to lack a sufficient police force to keep an eye on what James Crown was about to do.

Government officials showed him an expansive villa reputedly once owned by Robert Vesco and Pablo Escabar but subsequently confiscated by the state. The villa housed twenty-seven bedrooms, a large front room that could be easily converted into a reception area, and examination rooms. Because the villa's upkeep was so costly, the government was eager to sell the property. James Crown pronounced it perfect and signed an Intent to Purchase agreement that very afternoon. Government officials celebrated with him that night with a dinner that included the best caviar and prostitutes that money could buy.

The future looked bright for James Crown and for the city of La Chorrera. But our story does not begin there. It begins about a year later, in the small town of Villa Rosario, an ancient and dusty pueblo located eleven miles southwest of La Chorrera.

CHAPTER ONE

Dan Landes, as you may already know, is an American citizen, born and raised in the USA. He worked as a detective in LA for a number of years but took early retirement some twenty years ago and moved to Panama. So, he's an expat— short for expatriate, from the Latin, meaning "out of country." And, as you also may know, he lives in the tiny town of Villa Rosario in Panama. The circumstances of his early retirement are the subject of another story. Let's just say they left him with a sense of bitterness and distrust toward the American justice system. But his friendship with José Fernando, the chief of police in Villa Rosario, has, over the years, convinced Dan that there is a certain type of justice in the world that exists outside of man-made law. 'Justice' is probably the wrong word. Let's just say that Dan has come to believe in karma, in the inexplicable fabric of the unintended consequences of one's action.

José Fernando (or, don Fernando, as he is known to everyone in Villa Rosario) has been the police chief of Villa Rosario forever. He is a big man whose gray hair and moustache are dyed a solid black. How he got the job of police chief, well, that's *also* the subject of another story. But everyone in Villa Rosario believes that he was appointed as police chief after he killed a brujo—an ancient sorcerer— who had been terrorizing the town. That reputation has kept many criminals from entering Villa Rosario, so don Fernando has never disavowed it.

But our story today does not involve ancient sorcerers. Rather, it involves the modern sorcery of medical science. And if I might digress once more before I start this tale, I would like to expound a bit on the perception of magic. You see, what we think of as magical depends on our cultural place in the world. If you took one of those fancy cameras that instantly prints a picture deep into the jungle of the Amazon and showed it to some natives who had never seen technology, they would think it was magic. You could point it at them, take their picture, instantly print their picture, hand that picture to them, and they would be stunned. They would think you were a sorcerer. You, of course, would understand that the photo was just a form of technology that involved light photons and chemicals on paper. On the other hand, if you took a sick friend to that same tribe, a friend who was dying of cancer, and the medicine man of that tribe held a ritual with smoke and chanting, and then, when you got back to civilization, the doctors confirmed that your friend's cancer was gone... *you* would be stunned. You would think that that tribe possessed some magical knowledge that could cure cancer. The medicine man, of course, would understand that the cure for cancer was just a form of technology involving vibration and directed energy. Everyone wants to believe in magic. But what we call magic depends on what we think is normal.

I point this phenomenon out because it plays a part in our story, but I have digressed long enough. Let us begin. And just to remind you, this all occurred a year *after* James Crown bought his villa in La Chorrera.

Villa Rosario is a pleasant town to walk around in the morning before it gets too hot. And Dan Landes had the habit of doing exactly that. It was a morning ritual he enjoyed, walking through the open-air farmers' market in the Parque Central and seeing the different fruits and vegetables that the locals were selling in their little stalls, stopping to chat with people he knew, occasionally buying something... This little ritual gave his life some pleasure, gave his body some exercise, and often resulted in him walking near the police station, where he would stop in and say hello to his best friend don Fernando and maybe have a cup of coffee.

And thus, it was that on this particular morning, Dan strolled into the Villa Rosario police station. The desk sergeant knew Dan, and indicated with a nod of his head that don Fernando was in his office.

Dan walked down the hall and peered into don Fernando's office through the open door. Don Fernando seemed engrossed in reading some papers. There was the ever-present bowl of M&Ms on his desk. As was his custom, he was munching on them as he read.

"Que tal, amigo?" Dan asked.

"Come in, Dani," don Fernando said, putting down the documents. "Come in. I have just made a fresh pot of coffee. Help yourself."

"I do not mean to interrupt, my friend. You look busy," Dan said.

"No, not at all," dan Fernando replied. "I was just educating myself on this this drug semi... sema.... semaglutide. It is very interesting. It seems to work magic."

Dan walked over to the coffee pot and poured himself a cup. "Never heard of it," he said. "What does it do?"

"It is so simple. So simple and so brilliant. It just makes you *not hungry*. You take it once a week and you stop being hungry. Then you lose weight *naturally*."

"Oh," said Dan, "are you talking about Ozempic?"

"Yes, Ozempic... it has other names like Wegovy and Rybelsus, but yes, all these drugs are versions of semaglutide. It is a miracle drug."

Dan sat down in the chair across from don Fernando's desk and sipped his coffee. "I don't know much about it," Dan said.

Don Fernando got a serious look on his face. "I need to lose weight, Dani. My wife is beginning to complain. That is not good." He patted his belly and said again, "I need to lose weight."

The fact was, don Fernando was a big man, standing at about six foot three, and he carried his weight well. But he had always been heavy. He probably tipped the scales at two-eighty. His size was a definite advantage in his line of work—especially when interrogating suspects. Still, don Fernando didn't have what you would call a healthy weight.

"There's that new gym that just opened up here in town," suggested Dan.

"No, Dani. I cannot be seen at a gym. It is not good for my image. I am the chief of police here. I cannot be seen struggling to do sit-ups."

"What about a Keto diet? You know, lots of protein and fats?"

Don Fernando gave a little laugh. "Yes, I tried that. I *gained* weight on that program! No, Dani. My problem is not *what* I eat; it's that I am *always* eating."

It's true, Dan thought. Don Fernando did like to eat. There was always a bowl of M&Ms or other candy on his desk; and the little store down the street did a daily business delivering empanadas or other snacks to his office. And he certainly did like to drink. He and Dan would have cocktails at their favorite bar—El Balcón—several nights a week. Plus, he always said that his wife was an excellent cook. No, there was never a shortage of food around don Fernando.

"So this new drug could be the answer to my prayers," don Fernando said. But then he frowned. "There is only one problem: you have to inject it yourself, with a needle! Into your stomach, once a week... I don't think I can do that. I do not like needles."

"It's probably like the needles that diabetics use, don Fernando," Dan said. "It's a very tiny needle. You don't feel a thing. But the bigger question is: is this drug even available in Panama?"

Don Fernando smiled broadly. "Yes, that is the good news, Dani. There is a new medical clinic that just opened in La Chorrera. *They* have it."

"Really? Here in Panama?" Dan said. "I'm impressed."

"Yes, they advertise heavily in the gringo newspapers and on Facebook," said don Fernando. "They claim they have all the new semaglutide medications. Here is a flyer they were handing out last week in the mercado."

Don Fernando handed Dan a glossy flyer for the Crown Weight-Loss Medical Clinic. There was a photo of a smiling Jim Crown in a white doctor's coat, complete with a stethoscope around his neck. Behind him were several slim women in nurses' uniforms. The flyer offered big discounts on Ozempic, Wegovy, and Rybelsus. There were glowing testimonials from satisfied clients. Below the slogan "Slim Down with Dr. Crown" was the claim that the clinic worked with all major US insurance companies, including TriCare and Medicare.

Dan frowned. "How can they say they work with Medicare?" he asked. Medicare doesn't cover treatment outside the US."

Don Fernando shrugged. "I don't know, Dani. I have asked my nephew to check them out to see if they are legit."

Don Fernando was referring to his nephew Jorge Manuel who, because of don Fernando's influence in local politics, happened to be the police chief of La Chorrera.

"That's a good idea," said Dan. "And that leads me to my second question: are these drugs safe?"

"Well, according to this Wikipedia article I've been reading, semaglutide was invented in 2012. So, it has been around a long time."

"That's not a long time in the drug world," said Dan. "Are there any side effects?"

Don Fernando picked up the article from his desk and read. "Let's see... Wikipedia says that side effects include nausea, diarrhea, vomiting, dizziness, fatigue, headache, and something called stomach paralysis."

"Uh huh," said Dan. "Well, I would proceed carefully, my friend. With new medicines, it's important to investigate them carefully."

"Yes, Dani. But I really need to lose some weight."

"I understand, don Fernando. I could stand to lose a few pounds myself. But still, you don't want to fuck with your health."

"True, Dani. I will see what Koki finds out," don Fernando said, referring to his nephew Jorge Manuel by his family nickname.

"How's he doing anyway? Is La Chorrera keeping him busy?"

"Oh, he is so busy, Dani. La Chorrera is growing so fast. Koki says they get more and more gringo tourists every day. The city council is very interested in protecting those tourists, you understand, because of the money they bring in. So, they authorized him to hire more policemen. He has a big job."

"Well, he's up to it," Dan replied. "He may be young, but he's got a good head on his shoulders."

"There was a tourist from your country who died in La Chorrera last week," don Fernando said. "Koki was very concerned, but it turned out that this man had had a stroke. Died in his hotel room. Luckily, it was natural causes, not a result of a crime."

"Was this an older man?" Dan asked.

"No. Koki said he was only thirty-four. Traveling alone in Panama. Very sad."

"Kinda young for a stroke," Dan said.

Don Fernando just shrugged and said, "God's will, Dani. We never know when our time will come."

Dan couldn't argue with that, so he just nodded. He and don Fernando talked for about ten more minutes about local politics and small-town gossip. Then Dan stood up, thanked don Fernando for the visit, and left.

As Dan made his way back to his apartment, he once again passed through the Parque Central. This huge green area is really the centerpiece of Villa Rosario, with its winding paths, its open-air market, and all the cement benches where the people of the town could sit and chat under the shade of the tall palm trees. It was probably because of his conversation with don Fernando about losing weight that Dan started to notice all the heavy people in the park. He paused by one of the empty benches and just looked around.

Panamanians tend to put on weight as they age because, being poor, their diet is heavy in carbohydrates, but as Dan looked around, he was aware that there were an awful lot of fat people walking through the park. Villa Rosario was too small to support the usual North American chains like McDonalds, so he couldn't blame it on fast food. But it did seem to Dan that the average Panamanian was about fifteen pounds heavier than he remembered them being when he first moved here almost twenty years ago. Of course, he was quite skinny back then himself. And we all know how faulty memory is.

Dan shrugged. Still, he thought, for the second time that day, he could stand to lose a few pounds. He made a mental note to start watching his diet more carefully.

CHAPTER TWO

Two days later, Dan's morning walk once again took him by the police station, and he decided to pop in and say hello to don Fernando and get a cup of coffee. But this time, when he got to don Fernando's office door, he saw that don Fernando had a visitor. It was don Fernando's nephew, Jorge Manuel.

"Ah, Dani, Dani. Come in," said don Fernando.

"No, I am interrupting," protested Dan.

"No, no! We are just visiting. Come in and have some coffee," don Fernando insisted. "In fact, you're just in time. We were just talking about that new weight-loss clinic in La Chorrera. Koki has done a great job of researching them."

"Do tell," Dan said, stepping into the office and making his way over to the sideboard that held the coffee pot and a stack of cups.

"It is part of a chain of US weight loss clinics," said Jorge Manuel. "They are based in Florida, but have clinics all through the US, all managed by this Dr. James Crown. He founded the company and is the CEO. But most of the stock is owned by various investment banks and hedge funds. Evidently, this Ozempic drug is extremely popular in the US. This James Crown was the first one to start selling it on a large scale. His clinics take in almost ten million dollars a year in sales."

"Wow," said Dan.

"See, Dani? I told you this drug was good."

"Well, don Fernando," Dan said, "just because something is popular doesn't mean it's good or safe." Dan turned to Jorge Manuel. "So, what's this Crown guy doing in Panama if he's so successful in the US?"

"The clinic in La Chorrera is a prototype, a residential resort for rich gringos. His clinics in the US are smaller operations, just outpatient clinics, mostly located in strip malls or in commercial areas near hospitals. They try to undercut the pharmacies and private doctors. They make their money on volume. But the La Chorrera clinic is an upscale inpatient business. Tourists book a two-week vacation in Panama, stay at the clinic overlooking the beach, get training in diet and exercise, and receive their Ozempic shots. The patients pay one price for the entire two weeks, which includes their rooms, their classes, and their meals— although when they take the medicine, they don't eat much. The clinic also books tours and excursions for them. They can take surfing lessons at the Playa Grande beach or boat tours of nearby Taboga Island or bus tours of Panama City. Or, if the patients want to stay somewhere else, they can just be outpatients, and just come in for their weekly shots. This is the latest thing, you know, this medical tourism."

"I see," said Dan. "Then what happens after the tourists' two weeks are up?

"They go back to the US with a prescription, which they can have filled at any of Dr. Crown's clinics," Jorge Manuel explained.

"Ah, yes," said Dan. "That's a pretty good business model. Get them started on the medicine down here and keep them supplied in the States. Interesting."

"Yes," continued Jorge Manuel. "The clinic is doing good business here. All their rooms are full. The city council is very happy that they chose La Chorrera for this project. It brings lots of shopping dollars into our community. The council has instructed me to protect the clinic and their guests."

"Koki even went and interviewed this doctor," don Fernando beamed.

"Well, I *met* him," Jorge Manuel clarified. The mayor of La Chorrera wanted to impress upon Dr. Crown how safe La Chorrera is, so he took me to a meeting and introduced me to him. He is a very charming man. He showed me all around the clinic and introduced me to the staff. He was very open about his business."

"And best of all, Dani," don Fernando interjected, "he gave Koki some coupons."

"Coupons?" Dan asked. "Coupons for what?"

"Coupons for free Ozempic treatment," don Fernando said with a smile.

"Dr. Crown gave me three coupons, each good for a month of free outpatient Ozempic treatment," Jorge Manuel explained. "He said I could give them to three of my friends, or give them all to one friend who could use them for a total of three months. I don't need them, so I gave them to my uncle."

Dan looked at Jorge Manuel. It was true. Jorge Manuel didn't need to lose weight; he was already skinny as a stick. Then he looked at don Fernando, who was smiling broadly.

"You know, Dani, this clinic is very expensive," don Fernando said. "Only rich gringos can go there. But now, thanks to Koki's generosity, I can go for three months for free! The nurse will give me the shots; I won't have to inject myself. And best of all, it's very discrete. I can get an appointment and not have to wait in line. No one will see me."

"Well, that's good, don Fernando," Dan said slowly, "although I hope you will be careful. Have you talked with your regular doctor about this?"

"Of course, Dani. I am always careful. My regular doctor has been nagging me for years to lose weight. I told him about this Ozempic, and he thinks it's a good idea."

Dan nodded. Don Fernando was obviously very happy about his good fortune, and Dan did not want to spoil that. Yet, he did not share in the enthusiasm. It was probably because Dan was an old-school gringo, with a built-in suspicion of things that seemed too good to be true. He knew that just because a drug was FDA-approved did not mean it was free of unknown—and potentially lethal—side effects. He particularly remembered the so-called miracle diet drug Fen-phen, from back in the nineties, that got pulled from the market after it was discovered that it could damage heart valves.

"I've already made an appointment at the clinic for my initial screening," don Fernando said. "They will give me a physical, do a blood analysis, and see which program and dosage is right for me. You see, Dani, this clinic is very thorough."

"I'm glad you're excited about it," Dan said tactfully. "Good health is important. Is there an exercise component to their program?"

Don Fernando frowned slightly. "Yes, they have— what do you call them?—those bicycles that do not move?"

"Spinning?" Dan suggested.

"Yes, they have a spinning room at the clinic. The coupon allows me to come for an hour a day, seven days a week, to their spinning classes."

"I take it from your expression that that does not appeal to you," Dan said.

"No, Dani. If God had wanted a bicycle that did not move, He would not have invented wheels. Besides, I do not think my devotion to the good citizens of Villa Rosario will allow me to take time away from my official duties to go *spinning*," don Fernando said, pronouncing the word spinning as if it left a bad taste in his mouth.

Jorge Manuel gave a little chuckle. "You have *never* liked to exercise."

Don Fernando shrugged. "And that is why Ozempic is perfect for me," he said. "I can go to this clinic once a week for three months, get my shots, and lose thirty pounds without having to do anything else. That's my goal: to lose thirty pounds!"

Dan just nodded.

Jorge Manuel must have read Dan's face because he said, "You know, señor Landes... if you want, I can arrange a tour of the clinic for you. Dr. Crown told me I could bring any of my colleagues by and he would show them around and answer any questions."

Dan considered this. On one hand, it wasn't any of his business if don Fernando wanted to go to a weight-loss clinic. On the other hand, don Fernando had been such a good friend for so long... Dan bit his lip, but said, "I might take you up on that offer, Jorge Manuel." Dan considered how much time such a trip would take out of his day, but finally he said, "I think I *would* like to see this place for myself. So, yes. See if you can you arrange that for me, and just let me know the exact address and when I need to be here."

"Con gusto, señor Landes. I will be glad to do it."

CHAPTER THREE

That afternoon, back in his apartment, Dan sat down at his desk, opened his laptop and spent an hour scouring the internet for information on Ozempic. He learned that its key ingredient, semaglutide, was a genetically engineered version of a hormone that occurs naturally in the body. It was originally developed in 2012 and approved by the FDA in 2017 as a treatment for diabetes, but when it was discovered that it also helped the obese shed pounds, it suddenly became popular. By 2020, over four million prescriptions had been written for it. And then, when Hollywood celebrities embraced it and started touting it on social media, the drug's popularity skyrocketed even higher. It became so popular that it was in short supply the world over. The drug was also expensive, costing anywhere between three to seven hundred dollars a month. The Ozempic and Wegovy brands were injected under the skin once a week, whereas the Rybelsus brand was in pill form, to be taken once a day.

Dan learned that the drug worked by increasing the body's production of insulin and slowing down digestion in the stomach. These two actions sent a signal to the brain indicating that the patient was full, thus reducing the craving for food. Basically, as don Fernando had first stated to Dan, the drug worked by simply making you not hungry. A person who was not hungry did not eat as much, so his or her body had to burn stored fat for energy, resulting in weight loss. A person was basically placed on a diet without having to exert any of the usual diet discipline. However, weight loss on semaglutide was not immediate; it took time. Dan read how a person on semaglutide might begin to see some weight loss after a month. But to lose serious weight, like the thirty pounds that don Fernando was hoping for, would take a year.

Dan also noticed that all the official sites for semaglutide stressed that the drug should be used in conjunction with a proper diet and exercise programs, which were two programs that Dan suspected don Fernando would *not* follow. But Dan was most interested in the side effects. He read about the common side effects of tiredness, nausea, constipation, headache, depression, and stomach blockages. But he was more concerned about the uncommon side effects: thyroid cancer, retinopathy, kidney problems, and pancreatis. However, the causal link between these serious health problems and semaglutide was disputed. The most that could be said was that these health risks were *associated* with the drug.

Dan's hour of research did not alleviate any of his concerns about this so-called miracle drug. On the other hand, his reading had reminded him of the long-term dangers of obesity. He knew, that because of his weight, don Fernando was a more likely candidate for diabetes, heart attack, and stroke. Maybe, Dan thought to himself, being on a diet drug would be a benefit to don Fernando, despite the risks. Dan just didn't know.

Just as he finished his internet research and was getting ready to close his laptop, Dan got a text from Jorge Manuel, saying that Dr. Crown could meet with him tomorrow morning and give him a brief tour of the clinic. Jorge Manuel offered to have one of his men pick Dan up from his apartment in the morning and take him to La Chorrera. Dan texted back his agreement and thanked Jorge Manuel.

The next morning, a police car dropped Dan off in front of the sprawling villa that was the Crown Weight-Loss Clinic. A large sign featuring the image of a smiling Jim Crown was firmly planted by the open iron gate that led to the villa. Jim Crown had had the entire building painted a salmon shade of pink, trimmed with white and light blue. The entire building exuded a happy, playful aura. It was meant to impress newly arriving patients, and it succeeded.

Dan walked up the driveway and through the front door. There was a large waiting room with large comfortable-looking leather chairs. Most of the chairs had large people sitting in them, mostly women, but a few men. Dan looked around the room and estimated that there were about fifteen people sitting there. He assumed they all were patients of the clinic. As he stood by the front door surveying the scene, a nurse came out of a side door, called a name, and a hefty man stood up, lumbered over to the nurse who took him into the back area through the side door.

Dan walked towards the reception counter. On the wall to the left of the reception counter were eight framed photographs, starting with a photograph of a smiling Dr. Jim Crown, followed by photos of skinny women in nurses' uniforms. The receptionist was also a svelte girl with dark hair pulled back into a tiny bun. Dan wondered if the clinic only hired very thin women as staff. Dan gave her his name and explained that he had an appointment with Dr. Crown. The girl smiled and nodded and said that Dr. Crown would be out momentarily.

A side door opened. Dan turned and looked, but it was just the same fat man leaving whom Dan had seen step through that door a few minutes earlier. The nurse followed him out and called out another name. A large woman rose from one of the leather seats.

Dan stepped to the side of the reception counter but continued to talk with the receptionist.

"Are all these people also here to see Dr. Crown?" Dan asked.

"Oh no," the receptionist said. "They are just here to receive their weekly shots. A lot of people find it hard to give themselves shots, so we do it for them. It's a free service we offer."

"I see. And how do they get their shots when they go back to the States?"

"They just go to any of our clinics. They can fill their prescriptions and give them their shots."

"What if they don't live near a clinic?" Dan asked.

"Then we can mail them their prescriptions in tablet form, and they can take them at home."

"Ah," said Dan. "So... why don't they just take the tablets to start with rather than get any injections?"

"A lot of people believe that the injections are more effective," the girl explained.

"Are they?" Dan asked.

The girl just smiled and said, "I don't know."

Just then, a rather plump woman walked up to the counter and said to the receptionist, "Hello, my name is Laura Jenkins. I'm here for my daily check-in."

"Yes, Miss Jenkins, just a minute. I'll get the nurse," the receptionist said.

The receptionist stood up and walked towards the back, leaving Dan and the woman just standing there.

"Hello," Dan said and smiled. "How are you doing on this beautiful day?"

"Very well, thank you," the woman said and smiled. "And you're right, it is a beautiful day."

Dan liked her smile. Just then the receptionist returned, followed by a nurse.

"Come on back, Miss Jenkins," the nurse said.

The woman stepped through the door just to the left of the receptionist counter and walked behind the receptionist to where the nurse was standing beside a large physician's scale. Dan watched as the woman slipped off her shoes and placed her purse on the table and stepped up onto the scale. The nurse adjusted the different weights.

"You've lost another two pounds since yesterday, Miss Jenkins," the nurse said. "That's very good."

The nurse wrote something down on a clipboard and then stepped away for a moment. The woman looked over to Dan, and Dan gave her a thumbs-up sign. The woman smiled.

The nurse returned holding a paper cup of water in one hand and a smaller paper cup in the other.

"And here's your Rybelsus, Miss Jenkins."

The woman popped a pill in her mouth from the smaller paper cup, washed it down with water, and handed both cups back to the nurse. She slipped her shoes back on, grabbed her purse, and said, "Well, I'm off to spinning class," and headed down a hallway.

Yes, Dan thought to himself, this woman was rather attractive, with such a pretty face. And yes, she was plump, but still attractive. Dan watched her as she walked away.

"A lot of people are *very* afraid of needles," the receptionist said, nodding toward Miss Jenkins. "They can't even stand it if *we* give them their shots, so the pills are a blessing for them. They can start with the medication here and receive future doses at home in the mail. Miss Jenkins, for example, comes in every day, takes her pill and goes to the exercise class."

Dan nodded, but asked, "You dole out the pills, one day at a time?"

"Well, we like to keep our patients focused. They come in, get weighed, take their medication, and then join the various exercise groups. This way, they can't skip a day."

"And how do they pay?" Dan asked.

"Oh, we set up a monthly automatic payment plan with clients at their first appointment.

Interesting, Dan thought. "And how long does that payment plan last?"

The receptionist looked confused by the question. She furrowed her brow and just said, "Well... forever."

Now it was Dan's turn to be confused. He gave the receptionist a questioning look.

"Once you start on Ozempic or any of these drugs, you have to stay on them... the rest of your life," the receptionist explained as if she was explaining something obvious to a child.

Dan was trying to absorb that statement when suddenly the side door to the right of the receptionist's desk opened and Dr. Crown appeared. Dan recognized him instantly from the flyers, the photograph on the wall, and from the huge sign in front of the clinic. He was even wearing the signature white doctor's jacket and a stethoscope around his neck.

"You must be Dan Landes," Dr. Crown announced loudly, extending his hand. "I'm Dr. Crown. Police Chief Manuel told me all about you. Please come in."

Dr. Crown placed his arm around Dan's shoulder and ushered him through the side door into the back clinic area.

"Police Chief Manuel tells me that you have lived in this area for almost twenty years, Mr. Landes, and that you are the only gringo that the police trust."

"Jorge Manuel is prone to exaggeration," Dan replied.

"Still, any friend of the local police chief is a friend of mine. And, by the way, you have picked an auspicious day to visit, Mr. Landes, because, this morning, we opened our hundred-and-fiftieth clinic. This one happens to be in Saginaw, Michigan. Do you know what that means, Mr. Landes? It means that, as of today, Crown Weight-Loss Incorporated became the world's largest chain of weight reduction clinics using a proprietary system of semaglutide medication, diet and exercise training. We have surpassed Weight Watchers, Jenny Craig, and Nutrisystems in the number of clinics worldwide. Although, between you and me, Mr. Landes, I never considered those competitors as clinics. They don't have doctors, and they don't prescribe medicine. They're more like AA meetings; they're hardly competitors. But Wall Street counts them as clinics, and so we must play the numbers game. And why, you may ask, Mr. Landes? Because weight loss and Wall Street have a lot in common. It's all about image. So, today we can say we are the world's largest, and that's good. That's very good. Because, today we *also* announced that we are going public. Our IPO will be released in three weeks. Yes, indeed, Mr. Landes. This *is* an auspicious day."

As Dr. Crown was bragging, Dan was realizing he did not like this man in the slightest. Jim Crown was just another loud, self-absorbed, pontificating, rich gringo, the type that Dan had left the US to get away from. But Dan just smiled and nodded, and let Jim Crown continue:

"These are our examination rooms, Mr. Landes. You can see we have all the latest equipment. At a patient's very first visit, we measure body fat percentage, body water percentage, muscle mass, bone mass and bone density. We have our own clinical laboratory in-house, so we also do blood analysis here. Every one of our patients gets a complete physical, complete blood workup, and medical history analysis before we even talk about weight loss. Ozempic and the other semaglutide medicines are miracle drugs, to be sure. But they are not for everyone, Mr. Landes. We are a medical facility first, and a weight-loss clinic second."

And *yet*, Dan thought to himself, they are issuing an IPO based on their reputation as a *weight-loss clinic*, an IPO that would undoubtedly raise millions and would make Jim Crown a millionaire several times over. But Dan kept his thoughts to himself. He was on a mission to find out if this clinic was going to be safe for don Fernando, and he had to keep his focus on the task at hand.

"Jorge Manuel tells me that this clinic is a prototype," Dan said.

"Yes, indeed, Mr. Landes. Sometimes, people need a good excuse to start a weight-loss program. And what better excuse than a tropical vacation? Our patients can tell their friends and family they are just taking a vacation, come here for two weeks of sun and fun, and trick themselves into starting their Ozempic journey. This is not a new idea, Mr. Landes. It's a well-known fact that gym memberships jump every January because of the New Year's Resolution phenomenon. But then those same memberships get cancelled by June. And why, Mr. Landes? Because gym memberships *do not* result in sustained weight loss! It's a proven fact. The same with diet. Diet and exercise alone simply don't work with most people. And why? Because most people simply don't have the willpower. It's not something we're born with. It's impossible to fight against the body's natural desire to eat and be lazy. But with Ozempic and its sister drugs, we eliminated the need for will power.

"But to answer your question, yes, the La Chorrera clinic is a prototype. We have clients at all different income levels, Mr. Landes, and our goal is to have a product and a location within reach of all of them. Some of our stateside clinics are in poorer neighborhoods; they are strictly medication-only; but other clinics are in middle class neighborhoods and offer Pilates, yoga, cooking classes, etc. We design each clinic to fit a targeted demographic. And let me tell you, Wall Street loves that.

"But *this* clinic is special. We designed it for... well, let me be honest, Mr. Landes, we designed this clinic for the very wealthy. Our research showed that many of our wealthiest patients simply couldn't bring themselves to visit one of our walk-in clinics in a shopping mall. The wealthy have a certain pride, that often makes for a rather lonely lifestyle. Don't you think, Mr. Landes? All the more lonely if they are overweight. But that pride is really anxiety—they don't want to be seen, recognized, and judged. But here, they are absolved of all that anxiety by the power of anonymity in an elegant tropical setting. It's a beautiful thing, don't you think?
This clinic is the prototype we intend to replicate in other locations. We broke ground last month in Mexico, and we have already secured locations in the Dominican Republic and Aruba."

God, can this man ever talk, Dan thought to himself.

"Speaking of your poorer clients," Dan interjected, "how can they afford Ozempic? I've heard it's pretty pricey."

"Yes, it is. For a long time there was what we called the Ozempic price barrier. But as Crown Weight-Loss Incorporated has grown in size, we have grown in influence. We have negotiated with a number of insurance companies to offer subsidies and discounts to our insured patients."

"And what about patients who have no insurance?" Dan asked.

Jim Crown paused and looked at Dan. Dan wondered if this question hit a nerve.

"We have several programs for patients without insurance," Jim Crown said. "First, we have our own Patient Financial Center, which helps connect patients with insurance companies that will cover them—after a sufficient waiting period has passed. Secondly, we have partnered with Great Western Consolidated Financial Services in the US to help patients with financial planning and short and long-term loans. And thirdly, our team of trained doctors and nurses can help guide patients to less expensive medical alternatives. We try to find a medical solution that fits each patient's budget."

This last sentence intrigued Dan. He hadn't realized that there were less expensive alternatives to the semaglutide drugs. His impression from his reading was that the companies that had developed the semaglutide drugs had a monopoly on effective weight-loss medicine.

"Are there cheaper medications that are as effective as Ozempic?" Dan asked.

"The short answer is yes," Jim Crown said, "but it depends on the individual patient. Everybody has a different metabolism and responds differently to different medications. And every weight-loss medication works differently. Some increase insulin, so that you burn calories faster; some prevent the body from absorbing fat; some actually increase your metabolism; and others slow down your digestion. Ozempic has the distinction of working well with the majority of people. But, in fact, there are hundreds of different medications to choose from if one cannot afford Ozempic. Our mission here at Crown Weight-Loss Incorporated is to find the right medication for every patient."

Dan nodded and then spoke without thinking. "No matter what their income level," he said.

"Exactly!" Jim Crown responded.

Dan was relieved his sarcasm had gone undetected.

"No one ever leaves our clinic empty-handed because of their budget," Jim Crown added. "We keep our costs down and pass the savings along to our patients. In fact, one of the things that Wall Street loves about us is our dedication to cost control. We have exclusive contracts with pharmaceutical manufacturers in India, Malaysia, and Mexico to supply us with high quality medication. That keeps our costs down. We even have our own interactive website, where a patient can be interviewed by a doctor, receive a prescription for Ozempic, and have that medication delivered to their house the very next day..."

"Wait a minute," Dan interrupted. "you mean people can just order Ozempic over the internet?"

"Not without a doctor's prescription, Mr. Landis, no no no... but, that said, there is no reason why someone has to walk into a clinic to get a prescription. Our Crown Weight-Loss Website has over one hundred doctors on-call, all across the United States. A patient connects to us over the internet, fills out a questionnaire, gets interviewed by a trained professional, and then is seen online by a qualified doctor. And if it's appropriate, they will receive a prescription for Ozempic, which is then delivered to the patient's home the next day by FedEx. It's very secure, very professional, and very discrete."

"And this website is already up and running?" Dan asked, incredulously.

"Yes, sir. It's been in operation for over a year, and between you and me, it is very successful—very, very successful. Wall Street loves our telehealth weight-loss program."

"Well, I have to ask, Dr. Crown, why have brick and mortar clinics if someone can just get Ozempic online?" Dan asked.

"Because not every state allows online medical intervention. There are thirty states that ban telehealth prescriptions. It's a backwards Luddite way of thinking, I know, Mr. Landes. The world is going to be completely online within the next five years. But for the moment, we have to open actual clinics in those thirty states that don't allow us to prescribe medication online."

"I see," said Dan, but already his head was spinning. "So, you only build clinics in the states that *don't* allow online prescriptions?" he asked slowly.

"Well, we *open* clinics in those states," corrected Jim Crown. "Technically, *this*," he said with a sweeping wave of his hand, "is the first clinic building we actually *own*. And our Mexican weight-loss resort that we broke ground on last month will be the first clinic that we've actually *built*. Unlike McDonalds, Mr. Landes, we are *not* in the real estate business. We don't own any of the land upon which our clinics are built in the States. As far as the US goes, we open clinics in buildings we *rent*, because we know that in five years, all of the states are going to allow online prescription services, and we won't need any actual clinic buildings. But we believe there will always be a need for luxurious, high-end, tropical weight-loss retreats such as this one, and so we make an exception to building and owning clinics outside of the States. Besides, real estate is extremely cheap outside of the US. Not to mention, there are numerous tax advantages to running part of our business in foreign countries. If I might speak frankly, with the tax advantages of an offshore clinic, this place is more profitable than any of our stateside clinics."

Dan was still trying to wrap his head around the scale of Jim Crown's weight-loss business. "So... so, you think that within five years, your entire business will be online, except for these foreign clinics?" he asked.

"Absolutely. There's no doubt about it," Jim Crown beamed. "The only thing holding that back is getting state medical boards to approve our telehealth doctors. You see, the thirty states that currently ban telehealth prescriptions are mired in the past, where a doctor has to be licensed in your state in order to write you a prescription. But Covid changed all that. When the pandemic hit, the more enlightened states realized that they needed the advantages that telehealth offered in order to fight the pandemic. There was no reason that a doctor in New Jersey couldn't diagnose a patient in California by using video conferencing. Video conferencing reduced the spread of Covid. So, those states started to issue exemptions. If a Covid patient in California needed a prescription for Paxlovid, a doctor in New Jersey could write that prescription even though that doctor was not licensed in California, *if* that doctor worked for a telehealth agency that had a California exemption for the treatment of Covid. Weight loss is no different. Crown Weight-Loss Incorporated has exemptions for the treatment of obesity in twenty states and the District of Columbia. It's just a matter of time before we secure exemptions in the other thirty states. It's just a question of money, Mr. Landes. These provincial state medical boards don't want to give up the fees they make in the licensing of out-of-state doctors. Once they realize that we're willing to pay those same fees for an exemption, they usually see the light. We are lobbying very hard in those thirty states to convince them of the advantages of telehealth weight loss for their citizens. It's just a matter of time."

"Wow," said Dan quietly. "I'm very impressed." Dan was being honest when he said that. But what impressed him was not the scale of Jim Crown's enterprise, but his greed and ambition. He felt a little nauseous.

"Well, wait until you see our spa area, Mr. Landes. Complete with an Olympic-size swimming pool, steam rooms, jacuzzi, and exercise room." Dr. Crown said.

Dan let himself be guided through a set of French doors to an outside patio. His head continued to spin as Dr. Crown continued to talk.

CHAPTER FOUR

It was about a week later when Dan ran into don Fernando in the Parque Central. Dan was walking on the shaded sidewalk that winds through the large park.

"How do I look, Dani?' don Fernando greeted Dan effusively with this question.

"Um, you look fine, don Fernando. What are you up to? Where are you going?"

"I am taking my daily walk, Dani. Mingling with the great citizenry of Villa Rosario and getting some exercise."

"Exercise? Really? Well... good for you, don Fernando."

"Yes, Dani. I told the people at the clinic I did not want to be seen in their exercise class, and they said that I should at least walk two kilometers a day."

"Wait. What? The weight-loss clinic? You joined it?"

"Yes, Dani. And I've already lost five pounds. These drugs are amazing. I'm just not hungry, and I feel so much better. I even have energy to walk around. Life is good!"

"Wait, don Fernando. You're talking about the Crown Clinic in La Chorrera? You joined that clinic? When did you do that?"

"Four days ago, Dani. Best decision of my life. I should have done it months ago."

Dan just stared at don Fernando with his mouth open. "You... you've lost five pounds in four days?" he finally asked.

"Yes, Dani. And I feel amazing. I am happy. My wife is happy, and *that* is the important thing. Look at me—out walking in the park!"

"That is unusual," Dan admitted. "So, tell me more, don Fernando. You went there and they did a physical?"

"Yes, Dani, a complete physical. They are very thorough. But I skipped the blood analysis. I do not like needles, you know. And then, when they showed me the needle that they would use to inject the Ozempic, I opted for the pills instead."

"So... you take Rybelsus?"

"Yes, that is the name of it. I take the Rybelsus pill every day, and I am not hungry."

"So, you drive to La Chorrera every day?" Dan asked.

"No. That's what they wanted, but I said no. I mean, what is the point? That's an hour roundtrip. I can weigh myself at home. And I'm not going to do their exercise class. So, we worked out a compromise. They give me a week's worth of pills, and I will go in once a week to get weighed. I can live with that."

"Wow," said Dan. "Well, good for you. How do you feel?"

"I feel great, Dani. Truly great. Better than ever."

"Well, good. Very good, don Fernando."

"Now, I must be off, Dani. Time waits for no man. I have to get my steps in, as you gringos say. Ha! That is such a funny expression. Maybe I should buy myself one of those funny watches that tells me how far I've walked. Ha! I will see you later."

And just like that, don Fernando walked away, leaving Dan standing there.

How weird, Dan thought. On one hand, he was glad don Fernando was exercising. And don Fernando certainly seemed enthused about his new routine. And he did actually look slightly thinner. Still, Dan couldn't shake the feeling of worrying about his friend. Dan knew that don Fernando was concerned about being overweight, but it bothered him to see don Fernando embracing Dr. Crown's program so quickly. It was not like don Fernando to be so impulsive.

CHAPTER FIVE

It was one of the hotel housekeepers who found the body of Laura Jenkins unconscious on the floor in her hotel room at the Buenos Sueños Boutique Hotel in La Chorrera.

Laura Jenkins—as you know—had come down to Panama to be a patient at Dr. Crown's clinic. However, the rooms at the clinic were sold out, so she had booked a room for two weeks at the upscale Buenos Sueños Boutique Hotel in downtown La Chorrera. She had gone to the clinic as an outpatient for two weeks, and—as you may remember—she had a deathly fear of needles, so she received her weight-loss medication in tablet form at the clinic. She also attended the jazzercise classes, the spinning classes, took the catamaran exclusions to the nearby island of Taboga Island, and generally had a wonderful vacation. Her vacation had been so pleasant, in fact, that Laura decided to extend it an extra week, much to the delight of the management of the hotel, which was charging her two hundred dollars a night for her suite.

The hotel management was, of course, very disturbed that one of their guests had fallen ill. The fact that they had charged her credit card the full amount for her extra week did help to lessen their shock. Nonetheless, no hotel wants unconscious guests—it's just bad for business. So, they did the right thing and called an ambulance right away. The ambulance took her to the La Chorrera hospital where—because she was a tourist—she immediately received the full attention of the emergency room doctors.

However, despite the doctors' best efforts, Laura Jenkins died in the emergency room, without ever regaining consciousness.

Panama is so dependent on tourism that whenever a tourist dies, regardless of the circumstances, it is always treated like a criminal matter. It appeared to the emergency room doctors that Laura Jenkins had died of a stroke. Still, they notified the La Chorrera police department, and Jorge Manuel immediately took charge of the investigation. He was especially concerned because this was the second American tourist who had died in La Chorrera in less than a month.

Jorge Manuel went to the Buenos Sueños Boutique Hotel, examined Laura Jenkins's hotel room, and interviewed the housekeeper who found her. There were no signs of forced entry or violence, and the housekeeper told him that the room had been locked from the inside. The hotel's surveillance cameras showed that Laura Jenkins had not received any guests the evening before her body was found.

Jorge Manuel did not see anything out of the ordinary in Laura Jenkins's room. However, in the bathroom, lined up on the counter next to the sink, were more than a dozen plastic bottles full of pills. He picked each one up and looked at them. Some were vitamins or supplements. Most were prescription bottles from the US. Jorge Manuel recognized some of the common vitamins, but did not recognize any of the medication names on any of the prescription bottles. He didn't understand why such a young woman would be taking so many different pills. But he remembered his uncle don Fernando once telling him to treat anything he didn't understand as evidence. So, Jorge Manuel seized all the pill bottles. The previous year, don Fernando had given him a gift of plastic bags marked 'evidence' in big letters. Jorge Manuel filled three of these evidence bags with the pill bottles. He was glad to finally be able to use don Fernando's gift.

As required, he notified the US Embassy in Panama City. They sent a representative to La Chorrera to collect Laura Jenkins's passport and valuables from the room. The embassy's representative had the difficult task of notifying the next of kin. As often happens, when the next of kin learned of the expense of shipping a body back to the States, the family opted for the substantially less expensive option of having the deceased cremated.

Jorge Manuel was satisfied that he had conducted a thorough investigation. There had been no foul play in the death of Laura Jenkins. It had simply been her time. It was very rare to have tourists die in La Chorrera. But who was he to question God? La Chorrera was becoming a popular tourist town now, especially since the opening of the Crown Weight-Loss Clinic. Naturally, there would be a rise in tourist injuries, accidents, and possible deaths.

However, Jorge Manuel's self-assurance was shaken the following week when he received the blood work analysis from the La Chorrera Hospital. As was the protocol for all tourist deaths in Panama, the hospital had sent a blood sample from the body of Laura Jenkins to the Forensic Laboratory at the Ministry of Justice in Panama City. The Forensic Laboratory did a complete blood analysis and sent the results back to the hospital. The hospital then notified Jorge Manuel. He read the report and immediately called his uncle don Fernando. But the desk sergeant told Jorge Manuel that don Fernando was out of the office on official business, and so Jorge Manuel called Dan Landes.

And thus it was that Dan Landes found himself in Jorge Manuel's office in La Chorrera the following morning, drinking coffee, and scrutinizing a laboratory report written in Spanish. Jorge Manuel sat and waited patiently for Dan to finish reading.

"Well," Dan said slowly, "this person had a lot of different medications in their system... but the problem was... there was a combination of dextroamphetamine saccharate and fluoxetine in their blood... which are both drugs that are found in prescription medicines, but according to this report, should *never* be mixed together ... okay, so *that's why* the hospital was concerned when they read this..." Dan took out his cell phone and Googled both drugs. It took him a minute to scroll through the different explanations. Jorge Manuel continued to wait patiently.

"Okay, so fluoxetine is Prozac. That's a prescription drug that is used in the US to treat depression... and let's see... dextroamphetamine saccharate is... oh, okay, that could be Adderall... that's a prescription drug used to treat hyperactivity, like ADHD... basically, it's prescription amphetamine... hmm, that does seem weird that a person would be both depressed *and* hyperactive. But... let's see, what else do the Google gods say?... Okay, here's an article that says those two drugs should never be taken together as they can cause rapid heart rate, high blood pressure, and possible stroke. Okay, okay... so, Jorge Manuel," Dan said, putting the report down. "Tell me what happened."

"The hotel found this woman passed out in her room," Jorge Manuel explained. "She was an American tourist."

"What hotel?" Dan interrupted.

"Los Buenos Sueños," answered Jorge Manuel.

"Ah. Fancy digs," said Dan. "Sorry, please continue."

"She was lying on the floor of her hotel room. One of the maids found her. The hotel called an ambulance immediately, and the ambulance took her to the hospital. I guess they did some type of brain scan and said she had had a stroke. But they could not revive her, and she died. I have her hospital records here," Jorge Manuel said. He picked up a manila file folder from his desk and handed it to Dan.

Dan started to leaf through the pages. It wasn't until he got several pages into the file that he noticed the deceased's name. He stared at it in disbelief.

"This—this was Laura Jenkins!" he sputtered.

"Did you know her?" Jorge Manuel asked.

"Yes, kind of—well, no, I didn't *know* her, but she— she came into that weight-loss clinic while I was waiting for that goofball doctor. She was there to pick up her medicine. We chatted a bit at the reception counter. She seemed like a very nice girl."

Dan scanned the medical papers for some indication of the deceased's age, height, weight... something to confirm his fear.

"This must be her," he said. "How many Laura Jenkinses can there be in La Chorrera? Damn! That's so sad."

Dan read through the rest of the hospital's medical records and then put the folder down and picked up the blood test results and reread them.

"According to this, the amount of amphetamine in her system wasn't lethal. But because it was mixed with the Prozac, that's when it became deadly... Okay, has anyone checked out her hotel room?" Dan asked.

"Oh yes, señor Landes," Jorge Manuel responded. "We started an investigation right away. I personally went to her hotel room. It was just like the maid had described. Her door was locked from the inside. No one had come to visit her the night before. The maid was going to clean the room, and when no one answered her knock, she used her passkey to go inside. That's when she found the body on the floor."

"Nothing suspicious, nothing out of the ordinary?" Dan asked.

"No, señor."

"And did you do an inventory of her hotel room?" Dan asked. "Were there any prescription drugs?"

"Yes, there were many," Jorge Manuel replied. "I have them all right here."

Jorge Manuel pulled the three plastic evidence bags out of his desk drawer and handed them to Dan.

"That's a lot of pills," Dan said. "Maybe she was a hypochondriac."

"What is that?" Jorge Manuel asked.

"A person who thinks they are sick a lot," Dan answered and took the three bags. He opened each one, placed the plastic vials on the table and started to arrange them.

"Okay, well, these five are just different vitamins, and these two bottles are just supplements, so we'll put them aside. What do we have left? This one's for Alprazolam. No idea what that is."

Dan took out his phone and googled it. "Oh, that's the generic form of Xanax." He looked at Jorge Manuel.

"Um, Xanax is for people who get panic attacks. It calms them down. Okay, and this one here is just a prescription strength Ibuprofen. And this one is Cyclobenzaprine. I don't know what that is." Dan looked at his phone again. "It's a muscle relaxant. Okay. We'll put that over here with the others. This one is Lisinopril. Let's see... Google says that's for high blood pressure. This one is Atorvastatin. This one I know—it's for high cholesterol. And this is... Omeprazole... Google says that's a generic form of Prilosec which is for heartburn. And this last bottle is... ah, this is the Fluoxetine. Bingo. That's the prescription for Prozac."

Dan looked at all the pill bottles on the desk, frowned and then asked, "Jorge Manuel, you searched the entire hotel room carefully? You looked through he medicine cabinets and you looked through her purse, all her belongings?"

"Sí, señor."

"And there were no other medications, no other pills?"

"No, señor. In fact, the representative from the embassy also searched. These are the only medications."

Dan nodded slowly.

"Is there something wrong, señor Landes?" Jorge Manuel asked.

Dan gestured toward the sixteen bottles on the table. "There's no Adderall," he said. "There was amphetamine in her body—that's what reacted with the Prozac—but where did she get the amphetamine? It's not in these medications."

"Maybe she bought it illegally," Jorge Manuel said. "Drugs are a problem in La Chorrera."

Dan nodded and said, "Maybe."

He picked up the two bottles of supplements and looked at them. One was for Quercetin and the other was for something called CO Q-10. Dan read the labels.

"Or maybe one of these supplements contains some natural form of amphetamine. I'm not familiar with either of these."

He picked up the blood analysis report from the Ministry of Justice Forensic Laboratory. "Who did the analysis? Ah... it was Dr. María José Vargas. Yes, I remember her. She's very professional. Maybe I could call her and ask about these supplements."

Dan considered that for a moment. He had met Dr. Vargas on several occasions and always found her attractive. Rather than call her, he thought, maybe he should visit her. It would be a good excuse to see her again.

"What happened to Laura Jenkins's body?" Dan asked.

"It was cremated," Jorge Manuel said.

Dan nodded and said, "Of course."

"Señor Landes," asked Jorge Manuel carefully, "do you think this Laura Jenkins was murdered?"

Dan shook his head no. "No, there's nothing to suggest that. I think that she just mixed the wrong drugs and had a stroke, like the medical report suggests. But I would like to get to the bottom of this. It always bothers me when I don't understand something. Can you call Dr. Vargas's office and see if we could drop by there today and discuss her report?"

"Of course, señor Landes."

CHAPTER SIX

And so it was that two hours later, Dan and Jorge Manuel were sitting in the waiting room of the Ministry of Justice's Forensic Laboratory in Panama City.

Jorge Manuel looked at his watch and then spoke in a low voice. "We've been waiting for twenty minutes."

Dan shrugged and said, "This is the Ministry of Justice, my friend, and justice always moves slow."

Jorge Manuel did not appreciate Dan's humor.

Just then a uniformed guard came up and gestured to both men to follow him. The guard led them through a maze of hallways to Dr. María José Vargas's office.

There she was, sitting behind a desk with neat stacks of folders, just as pretty and formal as Dan remembered her. Her black hair, with some light streaks of gray, was pulled back in a tight bun. She had a totally professional look about her, but when she saw Dan she smiled warmly, stood up, and came around the desk to give him a traditional Panamanian hug and kiss on the cheek.

"Señor Landes," she said. "It has been too long. How are you?"

"I am well, thank you," Dan said. "You remember Police Chief Jorge Manuel?"

"Of course," Dr. Vargas said, also giving him a hug and a peck on the cheek. "Please, sit down, and tell me to what I owe this wonderful visit."

"Well," began Dan, "there was a woman who died last week in La Chorrera, and your office did the blood work." He handed her the report. "And we just had a few questions."

Dr. Vargas leafed through the report. "Oh, yes. I remember this case."

Dan nodded. "The hospital said that she died of a stroke. Your report suggests that the stroke was caused by the combination of Prozac and some type of amphetamine."

"Yes," said Dr. Vargas. "It is a very dangerous combination. Fortunately, we do not see it very often. But given the hospital's report on the cause of death and the chemicals we found in her blood, it's logical to conclude that the stroke was caused by the ingestion of these two chemicals. It's not definite proof, but it's a strong possibility."

"The police did a thorough search of her hotel room," Dan said, "and found lots of prescription bottles, including Prozac, but they didn't find anything like Adderall that might contain amphetamine. So, we're operating on the theory that this woman might have bought some illicit amphetamine, some kind of speed or meth, from a street dealer."

Dr. Vargas shook her head. "This was dextroamphetamine saccharate. That is, this was prescription quality amphetamine, not some street drug. That's not to say she didn't buy the drug illegally, but it was prescription quality."

"What about these supplements, Quercetin and CO Q-10. Do they contain any amphetamine?" Dan asked.

Dr. Vargas shook her head again. "No," she said, "this was pharmaceutical grade dextroamphetamine saccharate in her blood."

Jorge Manuel spoke up. "Maybe this girl did not know that you cannot mix these two drugs. Maybe some well-meaning friend of hers simply gave her this Adderall, you know, to pep her up."

"Sure," said Dr. Vargas. "It happens all the time. But... we may never know how or why she took both of these drugs together."

Dan pursed his lips. "Well, darn. I was hoping for an easy solution." He paused before speaking again. "You know, I *met* this girl—quite by accident—about a week or so before she died. I had gone to that new Crown Weight-Loss Clinic to interview the owner. She was there for her daily workout.

She seemed nice. A bit overweight, but so young to die from a stroke."

"Yes, I noticed her weight in the hospital report," Dr. Vargas said. "Obesity is a causal factor in stroke, but still, very sad to die so young. Was she at the clinic to start a weight-loss program?"

"Oh, I think she was already enrolled. She was taking that Rybelsus medicine," Dan said.

Dr. Vargas shook her head again. "No, Rybelsus is one of the semaglutide medicines. And although semaglutide is a synthetic version of a hormone that occurs naturally in the body, it stands out differently from that hormone. That is to say, synthetic semaglutide shows up in our blood tests. This woman was not on Rybelsus. Semaglutide stays in the body for a long time. We would have seen semaglutide in her blood if she was taking Rybelsus."

"I... I saw her take the medicine," Dan said. "I mean, the nurse gave it to her right in front of me. And the receptionist told me that with outpatients, they make them come to the clinic each day to work out, and the clinic gives them their daily pill."

Dr. Vargas shook her head yet again. "It takes a body about five weeks to clear semaglutide out of the system. If she was taking Rybelsus, we would have detected it in her blood."

Dan leaned back in his chair. He was beginning to get a headache. He looked at Dr. Vargas, and she looked at him. And at that exact moment, the very same thought entered both of their minds.

"Is it possible that...?" Dan started to say.

But Dr. Vargas finished his sentence. "Amphetamines are a cheap way to lose weight—a lot cheaper than Rybelsus."

Jorge Manuel spoke up. "I don't understand," he said.

"Your friend is thinking that this clinic gave this patient amphetamine," Dr. Vargas said.

Jorge Manuel's eyes widened.

There was silence in the room as everyone considered the implications.

Finally, Dan stood up, indicating it was time to go, and said, "Dr. Vargas—María—thank you once again for your time and your wonderful expertise. We have to go now. I really hope we're wrong, but I think I know where I can get a hold of some of these Rybelsus pills that the clinic is giving out. Can I bring them to you to analyze this afternoon, to see what's actually inside them?"

"Of course, Dan. Glad to be of help."

CHAPTER SEVEN

Sitting in the passenger seat of Jorge Manuel's police car, after leaving Dr. Vargas's office, Dan tried to call don Fernando's cell phone, but there was no answer. So, he called the police station in Villa Rosario. The desk sergeant told him the same thing that he had told Jorge Manuel that morning: that don Fernando was out of the office on official business. Dan pressed the desk sergeant: Had don Fernando called in sick, or was this a scheduled day off? The desk sergeant told Dan that all he knew was that don Fernando had called in early that morning and said he was not coming in today.

It was not like don Fernando to miss a day of work. Dan was worried.

"Jorge Manuel, let's go to don Fernando's house," Dan said.

Jorge Manuel gave Dan a concerned look, and then, without saying a word, turned on his police siren and lights.

The ride from Panama City to don Fernando's house in Villa Rosario normally takes about an hour and a half, but with Jorge Manuel's driving, and the police siren, they made it there in forty minutes. During the ride, Dan tried to reassure himself that he was just being paranoid. It simply made no sense that the Crown Weight-Loss Clinic would give a police chief amphetamine instead of Rybelsus just to save a few bucks. Why would they risk that? It was more logical, as Jorge Manuel had suggested, that some friend of Laura Jenkins gave her some Adderall to pep her up or to help her lose even more weight. It was more logical that Laura Jenkins ingested the Adderall not knowing that it could have a fatal reaction with her prescription Prozac. But still... Dan was worried. Maybe the clinic didn't know that don Fernando was the police chief of Villa Rosario. Maybe they were already losing money on his free coupons, and didn't want the expense of giving him Rybelsus. But Dan couldn't believe the clinic could be so stupid, so corrupt.

When Jorge Manuel's car pulled up to don Fernando's house, Dan jumped out of the car and walked briskly to the front metal gate. Unlike so many Panamanian houses, don Fernando actually had a doorbell on his gate, and Dan pressed it firmly. After a few minutes, he pressed it again. He was about to press it a third time when don Fernando came to his front porch and waved at him. Don Fernando put something down, walked outside, down the patio walkway to the gate to let Dan and Jorge Manuel in. He was dressed in old jeans and a T-shirt, both of which were splattered with paint.

"Dani, Koki, what a surprise, come in, come in." Don Fernando unlocked the iron gate and let Dan and Jorge Manuel in. "I've been remodeling the kitchen. My wife has been after me for years to do this, and I finally decided to tackle it myself. No need to hire expensive architects and engineers. Come in, come in."

He led Dan and Jorge Manuel inside the house, through the living room, to the kitchen. It was, to put it mildly, a complete mess. The appliances had all been pulled away from the walls; drop cloths were spread everywhere; paint trays with different colors and paint rollers were scattered in different places; one wall had fresh paint on half of it while the drywall was torn out on another wall.

Dan surveyed the mess. "What do you think?" don Fernando beamed brightly.

Dan turned and looked carefully at don Fernando. He was smiling broadly. He seemed exuberant. He had paint splatters in his hair and on his clothes.

"I got the inspiration this morning," don Fernando explained. "I'm going to paint these two walls today, and then order some new countertop tomorrow. Maybe even a new stove. This one is pretty old. And I'm thinking about replacing these windows, although I would have to hire someone to do that. But it's going to look great."

"It's a big project," Dan said.

"Yes, but an overdue one. I got up early this morning and bought and mixed the paint. Oh, and you see here, I've torn out this drywall. That's going to be a new built-in liquor cabinet. I saw the idea in a catalog..."

"Don Fernando," Dan interrupted, "we need to talk."

"Yes, Dani, of course, Dani. I am sorry. I should offer you something to drink. I've just so excited to finally start this project."

"Don Fernando, we came here to today to talk to you about an important case. We need your help."

Don Fernando stopped and looked at Dan. "Oh, this is police business? I'm sorry, I did not realize..."

"Let's go out to your back patio and sit down, don Fernando," Dan said. "We need to talk seriously. We need your advice."

"Yes, Dani, of course."

Don Fernando carefully stepped his way over the cans of paint, out through the back kitchen door, with Dan and Jorge Manuel following. The three men sat down at the patio table.

"I'm all ears, Dani," don Fernando said. "How can I help?"

Dan inhaled deeply. He had to figure out a way to engage don Fernando's police brain. "Jorge Manuel has a murder case in La Chorrera, don Fernando. It's not your usual murder case. It's a felony-murder case. We think someone gave drugs to a young woman, and she overdosed and died. Our evidence is not good. In fact, it's all circumstantial at this point. We have a suspect in mind, but we could be wrong. He might be innocent."

Don Fernando was looking at Dan intensely and nodding his head. He seemed to be focusing on what Dan was saying.

"We need your help in solving this case. In fact, we can't solve this case without your help, amigo."

Dan paused to consider how to formulate his next sentence. He felt he had to pick his words carefully. "Our suspect... I want to call him a drug dealer, but I'm just not sure yet. But he works at the Crown Weight-Loss Clinic. And we think, that—through some bizarre coincidence—he tried to hide his drugs in the medication that the clinic gave to several people, *including you*. We think the medication that *you* have from the clinic might be contaminated with some trace amount of this suspect's drugs. And we need your permission, my friend, to borrow your prescription for just a few hours. Dr. María José Vargas is going to analyze them, and if they are not contaminated, we will bring the prescription right back to you."

"I don't think my medicine is contaminated, Dani. It is doing exactly what they said it would do. I have been losing weight. I have more energy. I feel great."

"The young woman in La Chorrera felt great, too, don Fernando. She was happy and losing weight, and then suddenly she keeled over dead."

Don Fernando frowned but nodded his head. Dan could almost see his police brain working.

"Your nephew and I have been working this case all day, don Fernando. We can't solve it without your help. If we can just borrow your prescription just for a few hours, we might be able to solve this case."

"Do you need all of my pills, Dani?" don Fernando asked.

"Well no," Dan admitted, "just a couple of them. But try not to take the rest until we analyze the pills."

Don Fernando nodded his head slowly, then said, "Okay, Dani, if it will help the investigation, I will give you a few of the pills. But I need them back, you understand. I am losing weight for the very first time and I don't want to get off track."

"Don Fernando," Dan said, "I will bring your pills back this afternoon, I promise."

Don Fernando got up and walked back inside the kitchen. Jorge Manuel looked at Dan. "I've never seen my uncle like this," he whispered.

"I know, Jorge Manuel," Dan said. "We take him for granted because he's always so dependable. He's always there for us."

Jorge Manuel nodded.

Don Fernando walked back out to the patio holding a prescription bottle from the Crown Weight-Loss Clinic and a small envelope. Dan watched him pour two pills from the bottle into the envelope. Still holding the envelope in one hand, don Fernando lifted the pill bottle up to the light and looked at the few pills that remained in the bottle.

"Was this girl, the one who died, was she a patient at the clinic?"

Dan nodded yes.

"Was she taking the Rybelsus pills?"

Dan nodded yes.

Don Fernando handed the envelope to Dan.

"By this afternoon?" don Fernando asked.

"Yes, don Fernando. I promise."

CHAPTER EIGHT

As soon as Jorge Manuel drove out of don Fernando's neighborhood, he turned his police lights and siren back on. Dan called Dr. Vargas on his cell phone, explained what they happened at don Fernando's house and told her that they were on their way with the suspected drugs to analyze.

Dan hung up his cell phone and turned to Jorge Manuel. "I hope I'm wrong about this. I hope this is just a wild goose chase..."

"My uncle was, how do you say? Very wired up," Jorge Manuel said.

"Yes. And that's what worries me," Dan replied. "It makes no sense that the clinic would do this..." Dan's voice trailed off. He thought about his twenty-year friendship with don Fernando. Don Fernando had always been so steadfast, so consistent, so dependable. Dan couldn't imagine Villa Rosario without him.

Dan shook his head as if to knock these thoughts out of his brain. He forced himself to think like a detective, only moving one step at a time. First, analyze the pills in the envelope that don Fernando had given him. Those results will determine the next step. He had to stay focused and not get ahead of himself.

He tried to think back to the tour that Dr. Crown had given him. What was it Dr. Crown said? Something about having contracts with pharmaceutical factories in other countries? There was something he had said that left Dan with the impression that he was importing generic drugs from India or Malaysia or somewhere. Maybe something got switched in the manufacturing process. Then, Dan remembered all of Dr. Crown's talk about price control, on keeping costs down in order to make the IPO look good to Wall Street. Damn, Dan thought. Greed is such a motherfucker! But maybe he was being hasty in focusing on Dr. Crown. It was just that he thought the doctor was such an arrogant ass.

Forty minutes later, Jorge Manuel's police car pulled up in front of the Ministry of Justice Forensic Laboratory in Panama City. This time, Dan and Jorge Manuel were not kept waiting in the reception area. A guard immediately escorted them into Dr. Vargas's office.

"Here's what don Fernando gave me," Dan said, handing her the envelope with the two pills."

"Okay," Dr. Vargas said, "you two wait right here. I'm taking these to the lab. I should be back in about fifteen minutes."

It was an excruciatingly long wait. There was little to say, so Dan and Jorge Manuel simply sat, each staring at the all the reference books on Dr. Vargas's bookshelves, or the stacks of papers on her desk, or mostly at the floor or the front of her wooden desk.

Finally, she came back into the office with a piece of paper in her hand and sat down at her desk. Dan and Jorge Manuel just looked at her, waiting for the verdict.

"It's amphetamine," she said. "Each of those pills contained forty milligrams of dextroamphetamine saccharate, pharmaceutical quality."

"Damnit," said Dan under his breath. And then he asked, "And what kind of dosage is that? I mean, is that a *low dose*?"

"No," said Dr. Vargas, "that's about the maximum daily dose of Adderall you'd give the average adult. You wouldn't start off with that dose. You'd gradually increase the dose until you got to forty milligrams."

Dan nodded.

"But it's a good amount for losing weight. It *would* curb your hunger; you'd feel energized. Your sleep cycle would even adjust to it... as long as you only took one tablet a day. How long has don Fernando been taking this drug?"

Dan looked at Jorge Manuel. Jorge Manuel shook his head to indicate that he didn't know. "Let me think," Dan said. "I ran into him in the park about a week ago, maybe a week and a few days... and he told me that he had started at the clinic four days prior to that... so, I would guess just two weeks," Dan said.

"Well, that's long enough where he's become accustomed to the pills. That is, he's probably developed a dependence, but he's not yet fully addicted. I don't know his medical history, but a man of his age should not be taking them at all. How many pills does he have?"

"I think he told me that he goes each week to the clinic, to weigh in. My impression is that they give him just a new week's supply every time he goes in," Dan said.

"What I meant was, how many pills he has left?" Dr. Vargas asked.

"Well, it looked like he had two or three pills left in the bottle, plus the two we brought here," Dan said.

Dr. Vargas seemed to be thinking. "This is a delicate situation," she said. "Do you think that don Fernando would be willing to go to his private physician and admit that he's been using amphetamines and get some medical supervision for getting off the drugs?"

Dan and Jorge Manuel looked at each other and simultaneously shook their heads.

"He's such a proud person," Dan said. "He would never admit, even to his own doctor, that he was using, drugs. His reputation is everything to him."

Dr. Vargas nodded. "Yes, I know him, and that's what I thought as well. It looks like you two will just have to convince him to quit cold. First, you will have to confront him and make him understand what's going on. You have to take away the pills he has and make him understand that, medically speaking, he is amphetamine dependent. If he stops the pills today, he will have two to three days of unpleasant side effects. He will feel anxious, depressed, agitated, maybe even paranoid. He will crave the pills. He may have insomnia. Someone should stay with him. He will need to drink lots of water. The first three days are the worst, but he should be fine within five days. I had the lab print out a report of the drug analysis so that you can show him. He needs to understand the danger he's in."

Dan took the paper that Dr. Vargas handed him. "Thank you," he said, "I'm so grateful for your help in this. I promised don Fernando that we'd come back to see him this afternoon, so we'd better get going."

Dr. Vargas nodded, then said, "You have your work cut out for you. No telling how many other patients are taking amphetamines. Forty milligrams is not a lethal dose, but as with that poor young girl, it can be lethal if combined with the wrong medicine."

For the second time that day, Dan and Jorge Manuel drove from Panama City back to the town of Villa Rosario, with lights and sirens going.

"This is so crazy, señor Landes," Jorge Manuel said.

"Yes, I know. I just can't believe the clinic would do this," Dan said. But as he turned the matter over in his mind, Dan realized that any investigation against the clinic was at ground zero. There was no way to even prove that the clinic gave Laura Jenkins amphetamine. The only evidence they had so far was don Fernando's pills, and there was no official chain of custody for them. The clinic could always claim that don Fernando substituted his own pills in their bottle. Plus, the clinic could stonewall any subpoena and hide behind the wall of patient confidentiality. Any investigation would have to be handled very carefully and quietly. Dan shook his head. First, however, he had to make sure his friend was going to be okay.

Jorge Manuel turned off his police siren and lights as they entered Villa Rosario. He drove to don Fernando's neighborhood and parked his police car up in front of don Fernando's house. He and Dan got out, and once again Dan rang the doorbell several times. Eventually don Fernando appeared, with even more paint splatters on his clothes and in his hair.

"Ah Dani, Koki, you are back! Good. I have changed my mind on the paint color. Come in and look at the wall now and give me your opinion."

Dan and Jorge Manuel stepped into the kitchen, carefully avoiding the open cans of paint on the floor. The wall, which don Fernando had painted an off-white that morning, was now a light blue.

"Very nice, don Fernando," said Dan. "But we need to talk. We have much news on our murder investigation. Can we go sit on your patio again and get your expert advice?"

"Of course, Dani. I will make some coffee."

And so it was that for the second time that day Dan found himself sitting at a table on don Fernando's patio, choosing his words very carefully.

"Let me start at the beginning, don Fernando, so that you have the whole story. There was this woman. Her name was Laura Jenkins. Nice girl. But she was a bit plump, a bit *gordita,* and she wanted to lose weight, so she flew down here from the US to be a patient at the Crown Weight-Loss Clinic. But all the clinic's guest rooms were booked, so she stayed at the Buenos Sueños hotel in La Chorrera and went to the clinic as an outpatient. She had a deathly fear of needles—you can understand that—so the clinic was giving her the Rybelsus tablets...

"Just like me!" don Fernando said and beamed.

"Exactly," said Dan, "but unlike you, she had to report to the clinic each day. Evidently, she didn't have your power of persuasion. They wouldn't give her a week's supply of pills at a time. They made her come into the clinic each day to get weighed, to work out in their exercise class, and to take her daily pill."

"Yes, they tried to make me do that, but I said no. They tried to insist, but I told them I would just go somewhere else unless they gave me a month's worth of pills. Eventually, we compromised on one week at a time."

"Right," said Dan. "Well, this girl Laura was coming in each day for her pill. But what the clinic didn't know was that she was also taking Prozac. She had a prescription for it. In fact, she had prescriptions for a lot of drugs from her doctors in the US."

Dan paused for a moment, then said, "Now, I don't know if the clinic knew she was on Prozac or not. Maybe she didn't tell them. Maybe they overlooked it. Maybe they started her out on Rybelsus. I don't know. But at some point, don Fernando, I'm convinced that the clinic started giving this girl amphetamines instead of Rybelsus. I'm absolutely convinced that they were substituting amphetamine for her daily Rybelsus pill. And the problem with that is that you cannot mix Prozac and amphetamine! It causes a stroke. Which is what this girl died of last week."

Don Fernando had been listening intently. Dan could tell that he was thinking. "How do you know she was taking amphetamines, Dani?" he asked.

Because the Forensic Laboratory in Panama City found amphetamine in her blood. Here's the report from Dr. María José Vargas. They found amphetamine and Prozac in her system—a lethal combination."

"Okay, Dani, but how do you know that *the clinic* gave her this amphetamine?"

"Because, don Fernando, that's what they are giving you."

There was dead silence at the table. Everyone seemed frozen in place. Dan and Jorge Manuel were waiting to see how don Fernando reacted to the news.

"My... pills... are... amphetamines?" don Fernando asked slowly.

"Here are the lab results from Dr. Vargas," Dan said, handing them to don Fernando. "There's not a drop of Rybelsus in your pills, don Fernando. The clinic has been giving you *speed* for the last two weeks. That's why you have so much energy. That's why you are losing weight. That's why your mind is racing."

Don Fernando read Dr. Vargas's report. There was a look of disbelief on his face.

"Amphetamines, Dani?" he said. "I can't believe it." He turned and looked at the kitchen in disarray, then back at the report. "Who knows about this, Dani?"

"Just the three of us... and Dr. Vargas," Dan said.

Don Fernando nodded. "We can't let it be known that the chief of police got bamboozled by a gringo clinic."

"Of course not, don Fernando," Dan said. "No one will know. In fact, we can say that you were working undercover to get proof against the clinic. What we'll do, don Fernando, is have you continue to go there each week and collect your pills, but we'll execute a chain of custody on them, and take them to Dr. Vargas, so that we can use them as evidence in court. That way, not only do we have an excuse for why you were going to the clinic, but you'll be the hero for getting the evidence to convict them."

"Yes, Dani! I like that! That is a good plan."

"But first things first, don Fernando. Our priority is your health. You need to stop taking those pills."

"That is not a problem, Dani. I will give them to you. You know me—all my life I have fought against drugs coming into our quiet town. It is horrible that these... these people have tricked me into using amphetamines. I will get even with them! Let me give you the pills."

Don Fernando got up and left the room and came back with the Crown Medical Clinic pill bottle in his hand. He handed the bottle to Dan. Dan looked at the bottle. There were three pills left.

"How long have you been taking these pills?"

"That's my third bottle. I picked it up two days ago."

"Okay, so you've been taking the pills for two weeks and two days..." Dan said. "That's what we estimated to Dr. Vargas. She said that for that length of time you are probably not addicted, but your body may have developed a dependency on them, which means that you're going to be uncomfortable to just stop taking the pills. You're going to want them again."

"No, Dani. I am strong. I will not take drugs."

"Yes, I understand that, don Fernando. I'm just saying that it's going to be normal for your body *to want to* take them. I know you are strong enough to resist that feeling."

"What I really want, Dani, is to drive to the clinic and arrest everyone there."

Dan gave a little shrug. "Yeah, well, we can't do that yet, don Fernando. We need to build a case. And in fact, because of who they are, we need to build our case very carefully."

"What do you mean, Dani, by who they are?" don Fernando asked.

"Well, don Fernando, this is a big corporation. There's a lot of money behind this clinic. They are in the process of raising millions of dollars on Wall Street. Plus, they represent a lot of tourist dollars for the city of La Chorrera. Nobody is going to like it when we start arresting people there. We must have absolutely solid proof first."

Don Fernando shook his head. "Ah, Dani. I miss the old days. I used to be able to just beat a confession out of someone."

"Those days are gone, don Fernando. We will have to build our case slowly, and make sure it's rock solid. Next week, we'll put a wire on you and send you into the clinic to pick up your pills. If we can get the nurse to say the pills are Rybelsus pills when she gives them to you, that would be great. Then we'll secure them, take them to Dr. Vargas to analyze. And we'll always keep a chain of custody on them, so they'll be admissible in court. Then, maybe, we can have a little chat with the nurse who gave the pills to you and convince her that it would be in her best interests to work with us. Then we'll have someone on the inside, and we can find out who else is receiving these pills. Step by step, don Fernando. That's how we have to do it."

Don Fernando was nodding his head.

"But first, we have to get through the next twenty-four hours. Have you eaten today?"

Don Fernando shook his head no.

"Then let's get some food," Dan said.

CHAPTER NINE

Six days later, don Fernando walked into the Crown Weight-Loss Clinic, wearing a wire. Parked outside the clinic, in an unmarked van, sat Dan, Jorge Manuel, and Carlos Wang. Carlos Wang was don Fernando's computer expert, although at that moment, he was monitoring the recording equipment that was tuned into the microphone that don Fernando was wearing. Carlos was wearing headphones and was the only one in the van who could hear what don Fernando was saying to the receptionist. Carlos gave a thumbs up signal to Dan and Jorge Manuel to indicate that the recording levels were good.

Don Fernando walked up to the reception desk and said, "Hello, I'm Jose Fernando and I'm here to pick up my weekly prescription of Rybelsus."

The reception thumbed through a stack of three by five cards until she found one with his name on it. "Ah, yes sir, Mr. Fernando. The nurse will be right out." Then she pressed a button on some type of intercom system at her desk. A nurse appeared almost immediately, and the receptionist handed her the three by five card. She looked at it, looked at don Fernando, smiled and said, "Won't you step back here, sir, and we'll get you weighed in."

This was the part that don Fernando was the most nervous about. It's not that the microphone discretely taped to the inside of his shirt weighed anything. It was that since he had stopped taking his daily pills, he had stopped losing weight at the rapid rate he was before.

The nurse adjusted the sliding weights on the scale. "It's looks like you've lost half a pound since last week," she said.

"Yes," don Fernando said. "It's been a very busy week, and I didn't have any chance to exercise."

"You know, sir, doing the daily exercises is an important part of our program. We can sign you up for a daily aerobics class or a spinning class. That will help you shed those pounds."

"Yes, yes, I will do that next week," don Fernando lied. "I just have to get through the rest of this busy week."

The nurse smiled and said, "I'll get your pills, sir. Just wait right here."

The nurse disappeared and reappeared a moment later holding an orange plastic vial.

"Here you go, sir."

"This is the Rybelsus?" don Fernando asked. He wanted to make sure he got the nurse on tape identifying the pills as Rybelsus.

"Yes, sir."

"Uh, by the way, what is the dosage of Rybelsus that I am taking?" he asked.

The nurse looked at the three by five card.

"Three milligrams," she said. "Next week, we'll increase it to seven milligrams."

"I see," said don Fernando. "Is that the standard dosage of Rybelsus?"

"Yes, sir. Three milligrams for thirty days, then seven milligrams for another thirty days, and then, depending on your progress, we can increase the dosage to fourteen milligrams."

"Of Rybelsus?"

"Yes, Rybelsus."

"Okay, great. Thank you very much," don Fernando said and smiled. Then he walked out of the clinic back to the van.

Inside the van, he handed the vial of pills directly to Carlos Wang, who placed them in an envelope marked as evidence, sealed the envelope, and wrote the date and time on the outside of the envelope with his signature. The fact was, don Fernando had just promoted Carlos Wang to Custody Control Officer that very morning, and Carlos was taking his new position very seriously. Jorge Manuel then also signed the envelope as a witness to Carlos Wang's signature. Villa Rosario had never had a Custody Control Officer before, and Carlos was determined to preserve the chain of custody for this piece of evidence.

Jorge Manuel then got into the driver's seat and the van headed for the Ministry of Justice Forensic Laboratory in Panama City, where Dr. Vargas was waiting.

*   *   *

At that very moment, as Jorge Manuel was driving the van to Panama City, Dr. James Crown was on the phone arguing with one of his biggest investors.

"Look, Glenn. What's the problem? Our US clinics are doing great, and this prototype here in Panama beating all our expectations. We're at full capacity; we've got overflow patients booked into nearby hotels; our waiting list is now at thirty days. We can't be doing any better than we are. This prototype *is very* successful. What more does BlackRock want?"

"They want lower costs across the board, Jim. This IPO isn't going to sell itself. We need BlackRock. If they say they want higher productivity, then we have to give them that. The insurance companies have us in a squeeze; they've capped the reimbursement rates they'll pay for prescriptions. Some of the state health plans are threatening to cut us out of their plans if we raise our rates. So, you have to find a way to lower your costs."

"Glenn, I've cut costs to the bone in all our clinics! I'm using generics from India as much as possible. Half of my nurses in the States aren't even licensed. I'm pushing add-ons of vitamins and supplements to all my patients. I've renegotiated lower rents in North Carolina, South Carolina, Missouri, and Wisconsin. We've got a tremendously successful business. Can't they see that?"

"Jim, it's not a question of reality; it's a question of perception and comparative IPO values. You could have the most successful weight-loss clinic system the world has ever seen. But if your comparative valuation is not better than the latest bitcoin ETF, or the latest online money transfer payment processor startup, then the investment dollars are going to flow to *those* IPOs. Not yours. It's a new world on Wall Street, Jim. You're competing against IPOs that are totally online, while you're still weighed down with actual brick and mortar costs. You've got to cut costs to compete with these big boys. Look, Jim. It's not that BlackRock doesn't see how profitable your clinics are. They see that. They see that you've got a good business. I keep reminding them how Amazon was in the early days. I keep telling them that our profits will go through the roof when you go totally to online clinics. But they are skeptical as to how fast that will happen. They are not convinced that all the US states will move quickly to embrace our model. They want to be convinced that they can turn a profit *now*. Not in five years. If they can put their money into a bitcoin ETF and double their investment in six months, why should they put their money into Crown Weight-Loss and wait five years?"

"Glenn, we're lobbying those states as hard as we can. We're pumping a fuckload of money into those states. A lot of it under the table. They're going to come around and allow us to do telehealth. And when they do, we're going to control the weight-loss industry!"

"I know, Jim. I believe in you, and in your business plan. But I'm telling you that we've got to see a reduction in costs in order for this IPO to fly."

"Shit, Glenn! The only thing I have left is to start laying people off. And I'm already razor thin on staff!"

"No, Jim. You can't do any layoffs this close to the IPO launch. It'll look obvious. You have to find some other way to cut costs. You're a smart guy. Find a way to cut costs, and then announce some new semaglutide source right before we go public to create some buzz. We need to be perceived as innovative, in control, and on the cutting edge."

"Damn it, Glenn... okay, I'll try and come up with something."

"Good boy, Jim. I'll give you a call in two days. I've got a meeting with BlackRock tomorrow afternoon."

*   *   *

An hour later, don Fernando, Dan, and Jorge Manuel were sitting in the large waiting room of the Ministry of Justice Forensic Laboratory in Panama City. They had arrived fifteen minutes earlier, and Dr. María José Vargas had taken their evidence envelope, signed the chain of custody form, and told them to wait while she conducted the drug analysis.

The three men sat quietly, each in their own thoughts. Jorge Manuel was thinking about his town of La Chorrera. More specifically, he was thinking about what would happen to his town if the prescription that the Crown Weight-Loss Clinic had given don Fernando that morning turned out to be amphetamines. Who exactly would he arrest? The nurse that gave don Fernando the prescription? Dr. Crown? Was there enough evidence to arrest anyone? Maybe his next step would be to get a search warrant and see how much amphetamine was in the clinic. He would have to ask don Fernando for advice. And what would happen if he did search the clinic and found pounds of amphetamines? Did he have the legal power to close the clinic? Would the city council approve such an action? The weight-loss clinic had proved to be a gold mine for La Chorrera. The rich gringo tourists who came to the clinic loved to go shopping in town. They loved buying colorful scarves, pottery, and wood carvings to take back home as souvenirs. Local stores were showing a good profit because of the clinic. The mayor and the city council were very happy. If he closed the clinic, he would be the most unpopular police chief that La Chorrera ever had. People would say, "What's a little amphetamine? There's plenty of amphetamine for sale in the parks late at night? Why was he picking on the clinic?" Jorge Manuel felt worried. Maybe he would lose his job all because of this clinic.

Don Fernando was also thinking about the clinic. This was the inevitable result of progress, he thought, the destruction of a good way of life. La Chorrera and his little town of Villa Rosario had been quiet, sleepy communities for as long as anyone could remember. Then gringos discovered them, and tourists started arriving. And the tourists brought fast food restaurants, condos, higher rents, inflation, and now drugs. Gringos ruin everything, he thought.

Dan was also thinking about the clinic. If the prescription that the clinic gave don Fernando that morning turned out to be Rybelsus, then they were back at square one. If it turned out to be amphetamines, they were still at square one. They would have to do many more undercover prescription pick-ups to build a case. They would have to recruit overweight undercover cops to go to the clinic as patients. It would take months of careful evidence gathering. And even if they could prove wide-spread amphetamine distribution, they wouldn't have any proof as to *who* was responsible. No, Dan thought, they would have to get a person on the inside. Maybe recruit a nurse from the Forensic Lab to apply for a job at the clinic, to go undercover. It was going to be a tough case.

All three men were lost in their thoughts when Dr. Vargas walked into the waiting room holding the evidence envelope and a lab report. She sat down on the couch across from don Fernando, looked at all three men, and then said, "It's amphetamine. The same prescription quality and dosage as the other pills from don Fernando." She handed the report to don Fernando. Then she handed the evidence envelope to Jorge Manuel who signed the chain-of-custody form on the back of the envelope.

Dan watched don Fernando read the lab report and just shook his head back and forth. "Those bastards," he said softly. "They could have killed me."

CHAPTER TEN

The next afternoon Dan once again found himself sitting with don Fernando and Jorge Manuel. This time it was in the interview room of the La Chorrera Police Department, where they were talking with a very nervous Enrique Calvino. Enrique Calvino was relatively new to the La Chorrera Police Force. He had been a patrol officer less than a year, and his job consisted of riding as a passenger in a patrol car that drove around the park and through the neighborhoods in the afternoons and early evenings. The theory was that the presence of a police car driving around the local streets would be a deterrent to pretty crime and burglars. But the fact was that in his eight months as a police officer, Enrique hadn't stopped any crime, hadn't seen any criminals, and hadn't arrested anyone. He had just ridden around in the passenger seat, staring out the window, waving at the neighbors, and watching the world go by.

His father had urged him to apply for the job of a patrol officer, because his father mistakenly believed that a patrol officer actually walked a beat through the neighborhoods. He hoped that such walking would help his son lose weight. For this was the most striking characteristic of the young Enrique: he was overweight. He was not morbidly obese—not yet, anyway. But because he was only five foot two, he looked heavier than he really was. And despite his father's hopes, Enrique had only managed to gain more weight working for the La Chorrera police department, because he simply sat in a patrol car all day long.

But it was this quality—his extra poundage—that qualified him for a very special assignment on this particular day, which is why Enrique Calvino found himself standing nervously in front of his captain, Jorge Manuel, along with the formidable don Fernando, and their quiet gringo friend Dan Landes.

"Private Calvino," Jorge Manuel was saying, "we asked you here today because we have a very special undercover assignment for you. We have chosen you from all of our other officers to undertake this important mission because we have faith that you can execute it flawlessly. You have exhibited exemplary service in the department for the last eight months, and we feel it is time to accelerate your training, and to give you an advanced opportunity to excel."

Dan listened and tried not to smile. Jorge Manuel was laying it on thick, and it was obvious that the chubby young man standing in front of them was anxious.

"This is a highly confidential assignment, Private Calvino," Jorge Manuel was saying, "I cannot stress this strongly enough. The most important aspect of this assignment is not the undercover work itself. Rather, it is the act of keeping this undercover work completely and utterly secret. No one can know of this assignment, not your family, not your friends. Absolutely *no one* outside of this room is to know of the important role you are about to play in this investigation."

Enrique Calvino nodded rapidly and said, "Sí, capitán."

"We have complete faith in you, Private Calvino," Jorge Manuel continued. "And that is why we are taking you into our confidence. So, let me tell you what is going on. We have received information that the Crown Weight-Loss Clinic on the edge of town has been adulterating the prescriptions that they are giving to their patients."

A look of confusion passed over Enrique Calvino's face.

Don Fernando spoke up. "Do you know what that means, private Calvino? To adulterate a prescription?"

Enrique shook his head no.

"It means they are giving out bad medicine instead of the correct medicine," don Fernando explained. "They are putting the health and lives of their patients at risk by giving them dangerous medicine. We know of one person who has died because they took the bad medicine that the clinic gave them."

"Yes," said Jorge Manuel. "Someone at the clinic is switching the pills that the patients are supposed to receive. We do not know who, but we need to find out. And you are going to play an important role in this investigation, private Calvino. We want you to go into the clinic, undercover. You can use your real name if you want, but you cannot tell them you are a police officer. We want you to tell them that you drive a delivery truck, and you are out of town for days at a time. We want you to go there and tell them that you want to join their clinic. Tell them that you want to lose weight. They will give you a physical exam and ask you a lot of health questions. They will ask you all about your eating habits and whether you exercise. And you can answer all those questions honestly. You can just relax and be yourself. *But...* you have to tell them that you are afraid of needles. Are you afraid of needles, private Calvino?"

Enrique shook his head no.

"Well, you will have to pretend that you are. You will have to say that you cannot stand needles; that you don't want any shots; but that you heard that they could give you some pills to help you lose weight. You understand?"

Enrique nodded his head yes.

Don Fernando spoke up again. "There are only three things you have to remember: First, don't tell them you are a police officer. Second, tell them you are very afraid of needles and want pills instead. And third, tell them you work as a truck driver and are gone for days at a time. Tell them that you can only come in once a week to pick up your prescription. Otherwise, they will make you come in every day and take the medicine right in front of them. And we don't want you to do that, because the medicine might hurt you. Do you understand?"

Enrique Calvino's eyes were wide, but he nodded his head yes.

"We made an appointment for you for tomorrow morning," Jorge Manuel said. "Wear civilian clothes to the appointment. We will come by your house to pick you up at nine o'clock, and we'll drive you over to the clinic and wait for you while they give you a physical exam. We can't put a wire on you tomorrow because they will make you take your shirt off for the medical exam. They will explain their weight-loss system to you. Try to act interested. When they ask you how you are going to pay, tell them you have a coupon. We will give you a coupon tomorrow morning to take with you. They will give you a week's worth of pills. Bring those pills back to us outside. You understand the plan? Do you think you can do it?

Enrique Calvino bit his lip before responding. "Sí, capitán. Most definitely."

"You're a good police officer, private Calvino. We'll see you tomorrow."

And with that, Enrique Calvino saluted Jorge Manuel. He wasn't sure if he should salute don Fernando, but he did, just in case. And then, just to be sure, he saluted Dan Landes. Then he left the room.

"Think he'll manage it?" Dan asked after Enrique left.

"I think so," said Jorge Manuel. "Besides, it will be a good experience for him.

Don Fernando sat silent. He was still fuming about what the clinic did to him.

CHAPTER ELEVEN

Private Enrique Calvino managed to pull off his first undercover assignment without any mistakes. He walked out of the Crown Weight-Loss Clinic the next morning, holding a plastic prescription vial of six pills. He climbed into the unmarked police car where Jorge Manuel and Dan were waiting. Enrique handed the pills to Jorge Manuel, who immediately placed them into an evidence envelope. Private Calvino also had a slip of paper with an appointment written on it for seven days hence.

"Very good, Private Calvino," Jorge Manuel said. "You are obviously a natural for this kind of work."

Enrique Calvino smiled. His pride at a job well done helped him forget that an hour before Jorge Manuel had picked him up at his house that morning, he had thrown up from nervousness.

"Next week," Jorge Manuel continued. "We will send you back into the clinic. But this time you will be wearing a wire. You will have to ask them what is in the pills. We want to record them saying that it is the weight-loss drug Rybelsus. But do not worry, we will rehearse exactly what to say."

Enrique Calvino nodded his head slowly. He hadn't realized that this would be an ongoing job. He wondered how many weeks he would have to continue to do this. He worried he would not be able to handle the stress. Maybe he wasn't cut out to be a police officer.

Jorge Manuel and Dan Landes drove Enrique back to his house and dropped him off. Then the two men drove directly to the Ministry of Justice Forensic Laboratory with the evidence envelope.

"Do you think these pills also contain amphetamine, señor Landes?"

"I will be absolutely shocked if they don't," Dan said. "The bigger question is how widespread this drug substitution is. Are *all* the patients at this clinic getting amphetamines? Or just the ones who are getting the pills? The patients getting the Ozempic shots, well, those shots are only once a week; so I don't see how they could be substituting amphetamines just once a week and get any weight loss in those patients. Don Fernando was losing weight because he was taking those pills every single day..."

"Did you ask my uncle if he wanted to come with us today?" Jorge Manuel asked.

"He was busy," Dan said. "In fact, he's in Panama City right now, meeting with Judge Andrés Cordela."

"My uncle-in-law?" exclaimed Jorge Manuel.

"Is he?" said Dan. "Let's see: Andrés Cordela is married to don Fernando's wife's sister... so yeah, I guess that makes him your uncle-in-law. I've always said that don Fernando is related to everyone who's anyone in Panama. Anyway, he's trying to get Judge Cordela to give him a search warrant for the clinic."

"Really? A search warrant? That would be great! That would sure save us a lot of time," Jorge Manuel said.

Dan nodded in agreement. They could use a break like that.

*   *   *

Forty minutes later, Dr. María José Vargas met the two men in the lobby of the Forensic Laboratory in Panama City. Just as before, they had to sit and wait while Dr. Vargas tested the pills that they had brought. And just as before, she came back into the lobby with a somber look on her face, carrying the evidence envelope containing the vial of bills and a laboratory report that verified that the pills were amphetamine.

"The lab results were exactly the same," she explained to the two men. "This is pharmaceutical quality amphetamine. I took minute scrapings from each pill. They are all amphetamine.

She handed the laboratory report and the evidence envelope to Jorge Manuel, and he initialed the back of the envelope to validate the chain of custody.

*   *   *

On the ride back, Jorge Manuel offered to take Dan to his apartment in Villa Rosario, but Dan asked to be dropped off at the Villa Rosario police station instead. He was hoping don Fernando would be there with news from his meeting with Judge Cordela. If Judge Cordela granted a search warrant, it would make things so much easier. If this were the States, Dan thought, under these same circumstances, a judge would grant a search warrant in a minute.

But this was Panama, and things are never easy in Panama.

When Dan got to don Fernando's office door, he could see by the look on don Fernando's face that things had not gone well with Judge Cordela.

"I couldn't believe it, Dani," don Fernando explained. "He is my own brother-in-law. But he turned me down."

"What?"

"Yeah, he wouldn't give me a search warrant. I went to speak with him privately, you know, back in his office, because I did not want to announce our evidence in an open courtroom. So, it was just me and him. First, he tried to give me some bullshit about not having enough probable cause, but I pressed him. I said we have my pills and the undercover agent's pills. What more did he need? But he said he needed more. He said those could have been simple mistakes made at the clinic. He told me that this Crown Clinic had been pouring a lot of money into the politicians' pockets in Panama City, and that a lot of people would be

73

upset if he did something that jeopardized this business. He said that the clinic got a sweet deal on this La Chorrera property because Jim Crown promised that if this clinic was successful, he would build three more in Panama. He tried to tell me how many jobs three more clinics would give to Panamanians, and how it would benefit our economy. He tried to say that even if the medicine was not perfect, it was only gringos that were at risk. I said, '*I* am not a gringo and *I* was at risk,' but he kept telling me I had to look at the big picture. He said that if he granted a search warrant and no amphetamine was found, he would be in big trouble. Worse, he said, would be if he granted a search warrant and a lot of amphetamine was found, and the clinic was forced to close… he would lose his job for sure! I was so pissed, Dani. I asked him what kind of evidence it would take to make him grow some balls and sign a search warrant, and he said I would have to have irrefutable evidence of complete corruption of the clinic. I wanted to say that he had already given me irrefutable evidence of his own corruption, but I managed to keep my mouth shut and not say that. I merely thanked him and promised him I would bring his irrefutable evidence."

"Wow," said Dan. "That must have been a heated exchange."

"It was, Dani. It's a good thing we're related or else he could have thrown me in jail."

"What are you going to do now, don Fernando?"

"I need to think of something, Dani. I need to think of something."

CHAPTER TWELVE

And don Fernando *did* think of something—something good. He had not maintained his position as police chief for so many decades by being stupid or by accepting defeat. Three days later, don Fernando called Dan and asked him to join him for a meeting in La Chorrera. As soon as Dan climbed into the police car, he noticed that don Fernando's mood was upbeat, almost happy.

"Ah, Dani. I am so glad you could come. We have a beautiful day, and an exciting meeting to go to."

"Really? What's the meeting about?" Dan asked.

"You'll see," said don Fernando, smiling.

When they got to the La Chorrera police department, the desk sergeant directed them to the interview room where Jorge Manuel was waiting with a very large woman dressed in an outfit that was much too tight for a woman her size. She seemed to be bursting out of her clothes. It was difficult to surmise the woman's age because her hair was dyed a solid black and she had a thick layer of makeup on her face, but Dan guessed she was about forty, maybe forty-five.

"Ah, Ana Luisa," said don Fernando. "Thank you so much for coming in today." He gave her a kiss on the cheek and then said, "Ana, this is my good friend Dan Landes." Ana Luisa extended her hand, and Dan shook it and smiled.

"Ana Luisa has graciously agreed to help us with this investigation," don Fernando explained to Dan. "Her gracious offer is so important to us that I cannot begin to express my gratitude to her. But it is so like her to be so kind and giving, to help others in their time of need. Clearly, God has blessed her with such generosity."

Ana began to blush under don Fernando's lavish praise. She waved her hand at him to stop. Don Fernando smiled and said, "But it's true, Ana. We are at an impasse in this investigation, and we cannot proceed without your help.

Jorge Manuel was already seated at the table next to Ana Luisa. Don Fernando and Dan sat themselves down, with don Fernando situated on the other side of Ana Luisa, and Dan taking the remaining chair across from her.

As if on cue, an officer appeared at the doorway with a tray of coffee and small pastries. He placed it in the middle of the table. Dan and Jorge Manuel helped themselves to a cup of coffee. Ana Luisa helped herself to one of the chocolate pastries.

Don Fernando cleared his throat and began to explain the situation to Ana Luisa. "Ana, I hesitated for days before I called you. I did not want to get you involved in this case because you are such an important person in our family, and in our community. But I simply had no one else to call. This is such a complicated case, I hardly know where to begin."

Don Fernando paused to gather his thoughts, and Ana picked up another pastry.

"You know this new clinic in La Chorrera?

Ana Luisa nodded and said, "The weight-loss place? Yes, my friends and I looked into it. We wanted to go, but it is too expensive."

"Oh no, Ana," don Fernando said. "You do not need to lose weight. You have always been so attractive and curvaceous."

Ana Luisa blushed again and again waved her hand at don Fernando to stop.

"No, it is true, Ana. And it is also true that the clinic is very expensive. It seems designed so that only rich gringos can afford to go there. You know, part of the mission of the La Chorrera Police Department is to protect its citizens and its visitors, and that includes even the rich gringo visitors. We don't want Panama to get a reputation for gouging tourists, even if those gringo tourists can afford it. We want to know if the clinic is charging a fair price for the services it offers. We have talked to many of the gringos who are clients there, and they are very happy with their results. But they all complain about the high prices at the clinic. We all know that the clinic is selling Ozempic, and we know that this drug is expensive. So, we expect that going to the clinic will not be cheap. But it appears to us, at least on the surface, that the clinic is charging too much for what it offers. But our problem is that the clinic is very secretive about its billing practices. So, what we want to do is to send you there to participate in their program and to keep detailed notes on what services you receive and whether they are worth the money. We want you to take their weekly Ozempic shots, to participate in their exercise programs, to go to their groups, and to note whatever any additional services they try to sell you. This will not cost you anything. We have a coupon good for a month's worth of service there. So, you can go there for free, for a month. Are you interested in this? Would you be willing to do this for us?"

Ana Luisa wiped her mouth and nodded her head. "Sí, don Fernando, I would be very interested in this."

Dan tried to keep his face neutral, but his mind was racing. Where was don Fernando going with this?

"Thank you, Ana. I know I speak for Jorge Manuel and for all the citizens and visitors to La Chorrera when I say we are grateful to you for volunteering to help us. Here's what we'll do. We will pick you up tomorrow morning and take you to a doctor in Panama City, a woman doctor named Dr. María José Vargas. She will give you a complete physical and take a blood sample. We want to be sure you are in perfect health before you go to this clinic. Then we will drive you to the clinic. They will give you another physical and offer you different services. You can choose whatever exercise program or group activity that you'd like, but we want you to choose the weekly injections of Ozempic as your medical program. They use a very tiny needle—you won't feel a thing. They will give you your first shot of Ozempic tomorrow. After you are done with the clinic, we will pick you up and take you back to Panama City to meet with Dr. Vargas again. She will take another blood sample, and we will ask you many questions about the services that the clinic offered you and what the prices were. It will be a very busy day tomorrow. Can you handle that?"

Ana Luisa nodded yes as she reached for another pastry. "Sí, don Fernando, I am glad to help, and I think it would be good for me."

Oh my God, Dan thought to himself. Don Fernando is using this woman as a guinea pig! He's sending her blind into the clinic so that he can test her blood to see what the clinic is putting into its Ozempic shots! Dan felt his heart begin to race. This is not right! What if the clinic is putting amphetamine into their shots? He's risking her health, and she has no idea!

Don Fernando was continuing to talk to Ana Luisa. "Gracias, Ana Luisa. We are so grateful for your help. Now, it is very important that we keep this investigation secret. We do not want to jeopardize the good work that the clinic is doing. We only want to be sure that they are treating all of their clients fairly and not overcharging them. But we don't want anyone to know that we are doing this. So, it is very important that you keep this investigation very secret. No one must know. Not your friends, not your family, no one!"

Ana Luisa nodded her head in agreement. Dan bit the inside of his cheek. He felt that he should say something, that he should somehow stop this from happening. But don Fernando was already standing up to give this woman a hug. Dan looked at Jorge Manuel, but he had also stood up to give the woman a hug. Dan stood up, almost involuntarily. Jorge Manuel escorted the woman out the door, telling her that one of his officers would give her a ride home.

Don Fernando sat down, looked at Dan and smiled. He seemed very satisfied.

"Don Fernando," Dan blurted out, "you can't do this!"

"Why not, Dani? What is the problem?"

"She's going in there blind, don Fernando! She has no idea what they will be injecting into her!"

"Well, neither do any of the other patients who go there," said don Fernando. "No one knows what they are being injected with. The clinic says it is using Ozempic. We just have to trust them. The city council of La Chorrera trusts them. The politicians in Panama City trust them. Why should we be any different?"

"That's bullshit, don Fernando. You're sending her in there to find out what medicine the clinic is using. They could be giving her amphetamine!"

"Oh, I don't think so Dani. People are losing a lot of weight there. A once-a-week injection of amphetamine would not cause such weight loss. I do not think Ana will receive amphetamine."

"But the point is, don Fernando, that you are sending her in there to find out what the clinic *is* using. You should have told her that!"

"Why, Dani? It would only stress her out. If the clinic is using Ozempic, then she will receive exactly what she expects to receive. If the clinic is not using Ozempic, then we will know right away and be able to stop them. Dr. Vargas will be waiting for us in Panama City. As soon as Ana Luisa gets her shot, we will take her to Dr. Vargas for a blood test. If the blood test shows that the clinic is not using Ozempic, then we can go straight to Judge André Cordela and get a search warrant for the clinic."

Dan shook his head in frustration. "The judge wouldn't give you a search warrant when we had proof that the clinic gave *you* amphetamine! He wouldn't give you a search warrant when we had proof that they gave Enrique Calvino amphetamine! What makes you think the judge will give you a search warrant this time?"

Don Fernando smiled and said, "Because Ana Luisa is Judge Cordela's daughter."

Dan stared at don Fernando, trying to take this information in.

"Judge Cordela said he needed irrefutable proof before he would issue a search warrant," don Fernando said. "Well, Dani, there is nothing more irrefutable than one's own family. Especially one's own daughter. If the clinic gives Ana Luisa anything other than Ozempic, I guarantee that Judge Cordela will grant me a search warrant. And if they give her Ozempic, well hey, no one is the wiser. It is—how do they say in your country?—no harm, no foul. But... if the clinic gives her something other than Ozempic, I will be able to shut those bastards down!"

Dan leaned back in his chair. He felt that the wind had been knocked out of him. "But don Fernando, she should know," he said weakly.

"God will protect her," don Fernando said. "She'll be fine. Come on, Dani, it's almost noon. Let's go get some lunch."

CHAPTER THIRTEEN

The next morning, as promised, don Fernando picked up Ana Luisa at her house and drove her to Panama City. Dr. Vargas met them at the Ministry of Justice Forensic Laboratory. Don Fernando explained the location to Ana Luisa by saying that Dr. Vargas was a friend and was volunteering her time for this project. Dr. Vargas gave Ana a complete physical, took her blood pressure, drew a blood sample, and asked her many questions about her medical history. Then don Fernando drove Ana to the Crown Weight-Loss Clinic for her appointment. At the clinic Ana was also given a physical exam, although it was a much briefer exam than the one Dr. Vargas had given her. The clinic nurse did take her blood pressure but did not take a blood sample, and only asked her a few questions about her medical history. Ana Luisa signed up for the daily Zumba class. She was very excited and a little nervous about losing weight. She had been fat all her life and had tried all the diets. Maybe this time, she hoped, she could slim down and look attractive.

Ana said she wanted to try the Ozempic program, and the nurse agreed that Ozempic would be a good fit for her. Ana presented her coupon for a free month of treatment, and the nurse gave her an injection. She had to wait fifteen minutes in the clinic to be sure that there was no allergic reaction to the injection, but then she was free to leave.

"See you in the Zumba class tomorrow," the nurse said as Ana was leaving.

Ana walked out to the car where don Fernando was waiting. He drove her back to Panama City where Dr. Vargas took another blood sample. Both Dr. Vargas and don Fernando asked her many questions about what happened at the clinic. All in all, for Ana Luisa, the experience had been a good one, and she was happy.

On the drive back to Villa Rosario, Ana Luisa opened up to don Fernando about her lifelong problem with weight.

"The worst was high school, uncle," she said. "All the other girls had dates on Saturday nights while I stayed home and helped my mama prepare the food for dinner. That's all I remember about every Saturday night in high school: preparing food with my mother."

"I understand, Ana Luisa. I understand," don Fernando said.

"And clothes, uncle, pretty clothes for a plus woman are so hard to find. The stores in Villa Rosario have clothes in my size, but they are not pretty. I order all my clothes online, and even then, I have to send half of them back because they don't fit. If this clinic can help me lose weight, I will buy all new clothes. Maybe then I can find a husband while I am still young."

Don Fernando just nodded. He had his own memories of being an overweight teenager.

He dropped Ana Luisa off at her house and again thanked her profusely for her help. Then he drove to the Villa Rosario Police Station. He knew he was behind on his paperwork and was hoping to get caught up. But when he arrived there, a terse message from Dr. Vargas was waiting for him. It simply said that she was on her way to Villa Rosario, asking if she could meet with him and Dan and Jorge Manuel. This did not sound good. He called both Dan and his nephew to come to his office.

Thirty minutes later, don Fernando, Dan and Jorge Manuel were sitting in the conference room of the police station when the desk sergeant brought Dr. Vargas in.

All three men started to stand up, but Dr. Vargas motioned them to remain seated. She then took a seat at the head of the table. She was all business.

"Gentlemen," she said, "when I got the laboratory results on the young woman that don Fernando brought to my office this morning, I was shocked, and I had to come her in person to talk with you. This is a forty-three-year-old woman with no history of diabetes. She is overweight, but her blood sugar levels are normal. She is not even pre-diabetic. The first blood test we ran on her this morning was completely normal, almost perfect. Then don Fernando took her to this weight-loss clinic where she received an injection, supposedly of Ozempic. But, as I've explained to Dan Landes a few weeks ago, Ozempic stays in your system a long time, and we can easily do a lab test for it. This woman did *not* receive Ozempic at this clinic this morning. There was no Ozempic or *any* semaglutide drug in her system. But, what there was in her system was an elevated amount of *insulin*. As I mentioned, she is not diabetic; she *does not* take insulin; she ate a normal breakfast before coming to my lab for her first visit this morning, and she did not eat anything between that time and coming back to see me after going to the clinic..."

Dr. Vargas paused, then said, "What the clinic is injecting their patients with is *insulin*, not Ozempic."

All three men looked at each other.

"Insulin is actually difficult to detect in the blood. The first tests we ran when this woman came back from the clinic showed nothing new in her blood compared to the tests we ran before she went to the clinic. This confused us, because we knew that the clinic had injected her with *something*. But we did notice that her blood sugar was low. So, we started doing more refined testing. That's when we discovered the extra insulin."

Dr. Vargas paused and looked at Jorge Manuel. He had a confused look on his face. She decided she needed to add some background. "Insulin is a hormone that our bodies make to regulate the amount of glucose, or blood sugar, in our blood and keep it in normal range. When a person can't produce enough natural insulin, or when they are resistant to their natural insulin, we call them diabetic. They need to take extra insulin. When a diabetic takes insulin, there is not any weight loss; the insulin simply returns the body to normal functioning. However, for someone who is *not* diabetic, taking additional insulin has a different effect: it suppresses the production of a hormone called ghrelin in the stomach. And ghrelin is the hormone that signals the brain when you are hungry. So, when a non-diabetic takes insulin, he or she is not hungry. So, they eat less and lose weight."

"Why would the clinic give their patients insulin?" Jorge Manuel asked.

Dan spoke up. "Because it's cheaper than Ozempic."

"Exactly," said Dr. Vargas. "Not only is it cheaper, but the side effects can mimic the side effects of Ozempic. A nondiabetic taking insulin might feel nauseous; they might feel tired. But they would just think that was the normal side effect of the Ozempic. And as I said, detecting extra insulin in the blood is difficult unless you are looking for it.

"And the risks to the patient?" don Fernando asked.

"It depends on the individual. In large doses, insulin can be fatal. The person can go into a coma. But the clinic did not give this woman a large dose. So I think the worst that she can expect is to feel dizzy, irritable, or tired. She could experience a rapid heartbeat. I saw her an hour after her injection, and she seemed okay. Still, this is a very dangerous and illegal practice. It can kill someone. This clinic needs to be shut down."

Don Fernando nodded. He looked worried. Dr. Vargas noticed that. "I think this particular patient will be alright, don Fernando. Just don't let her get any more injections from that clinic."

Dr. Vargas looked around the room. "Gentlemen, that's all I have. I came here as quickly as I could because I wanted you all to know what was going on. But if there are no more questions, I'll be on my way. Don Fernando, here are the laboratory tests on that woman and my report."

She handed a stack of papers to don Fernando and then left the room. Don Fernando leafed through the papers and pursed his lips. Dan leaned back in his chair and pondered the situation.

CHAPTER FOURTEEN

As Don Fernando predicted, he had no problem getting a search warrant from Judge Cordela the next morning. But the judge made him promise to be as discrete with the search as possible. Don Fernando waited until five o'clock that afternoon, which was the hour when the clinic usually closed. He showed up with five of his officers in plain clothes. Even then, they sat quietly in the waiting room until the last patient had left. Then don Fernando presented the stunned receptionist with the court order, and the five officers entered the back area of the clinic and started to inventory and seize samples of every different medication in the clinic's pharmacy.

Dr. Jim Crown was, of course, livid. He came out screaming and tried to block the officers. But, as mentioned, don Fernando is a rather large man, and he simply picked up the flailing Jim Crown, carried him out to the waiting room, sat him down in a chair and told him if he opened his mouth again, he would be arrested.

The whole operation took less than thirty minutes. The five officers loaded up a van with twelve boxes of different medicines—samples from every type of drug that was in the clinic's pharmacy. Don Fernando gave the furious Jim Crown a receipt for the twelve boxes, and the van sped away to Panama City, where Dr. Vargas was waiting.

The next morning, the clinic was open for business as usual. Dr. Crown had instructed the staff to say absolutely nothing to the patients, or else they would be fired. And since the local newspapers had not gotten wind of the search, none of the clinic's patients had any idea what had happened the night before. Jim Crown had to cancel all his medical appointments, however. He spent the morning on the phone with his personal lawyer back in New York City. Jim kept explaining that he had no idea what chemicals might actually be in the boxes of medications that the police seized. After all, he had ordered these medicines from reputable drug manufacturers in India, Malaysia, Turkey and Mexico. It wouldn't be his fault if some of the shipments were contaminated. The only thing he was guilty of, he explained, was trusting his suppliers. He and his lawyer decided not to tell any of the investors behind Crown Weight-Loss Incorporated about the police raid. No sense in jeopardizing the upcoming IPO. They also decided that if somehow the news did leak out, Jim Crown was going to play it off as just a typical third-world bureaucratic event—just another normal administrative hassle of running a clinic in a foreign country. By that afternoon, Jim Crown was feeling better.

But on that same afternoon, don Fernando was not feeling better. He was sitting in a conference room in the Ministry of Justice Forensic Laboratory with Dan and Dr. Vargas.

"I have some preliminary results," Dr. Vargas was saying. "We haven't tested all the samples, but what we have found so far is very disturbing. Two of the boxes labeled Ozempic were in fact Ozempic. They appear to be legitimate products from the original manufacturer, the Danish pharmaceutical company Novo Nordisk. But several other boxes of injectable needles were labeled Ozempic and, in fact, contained some form of semaglutide, but they were not Ozempic. They appear to be counterfeit Ozempic, sourced from non-licensed pharmaceutical manufacturers. We found some markings on the boxes that suggest they came from India. Three of the boxes of injectable needles were labeled Ozempic, but actually contained insulin. We've just started analyzing the boxes labeled Rybelsus, but so far, all of the samples we've taken have tested positive for amphetamine."

The room was quiet for a moment, then Dan said quietly. "In other words, the fraud here is systemic."

"Yes," agreed Dr. Vargas. "If we extrapolate from the samples we've tested, I would say that eighty percent of the clinic's patients are receiving counterfeit or illicit drugs. They are probably only giving the real Ozempic to their ultra-wealthy clients to take back to the States. It looks like everyone else receives either counterfeit or off-brand semaglutide products, or insulin, or amphetamine."

"I wonder if this fraud is just confined to this one clinic, or whether this is going on in all the other clinics in the US," Dan said.

Dr. Vargas shrugged. "I don't know."

Don Fernando shook his head. "I want to close them down," he said.

Dan folded his arms and asked, "How would you do that, don Fernando?"

"I will arrest this doctor and all his staff."

"I don't think you can do that," said Dan. "First of all, you have no proof as to who actually knows these drugs are counterfeit. The nurses could be giving out illicit drugs without even knowing it. Even though we have all this evidence, we don't know how many people in the clinic are participating in this fraud. Second, if you arrest Jim Crown, he'll just lawyer up and blame the suppliers. This is a big corporation, don Fernando. There are millions of dollars behind this clinic. If you arrest anyone, La Chorrera will be swarming with lawyers within two hours. There's a reason Judge Cordela wouldn't give you a search warrant when you first asked him."

"They need to be stopped," Dr. Vargas said.

"I agree," agreed Dan, "but you can't stop them by arresting them now. They'll make bail and be back in business the next day, blaming the pharmaceutical manufacturers and promising to test all their medicines before giving them to patients. And you'll be tied up in court for the next six months, answering motions and being subpoenaed for depositions."

"Then how? How can I stop them?" asked don Fernando.

"I think you need to proceed strategically," Dan said. "Have you noticed that you haven't heard a single complaint from the clinic about yesterday's raid? No lawyer has called you. Jim Crown's not complaining to the media. He's keeping quiet about the raid. And why? Because he's waiting for you to make the next move. But your best move is to not to make a move."

"How do I do that, Dani?"

"Don't you have that nephew who works for that big newspaper in Panama City?" Dan asked.

Don Fernando nodded yes.

"Well," Dan continued, "I think you need to work that relationship so that you can start leaking stories to him that he can publish. Start with unconfirmed reports that counterfeit Ozempic is finding its way into Panama. Then, a few days later, maybe a story that says that patients at the clinic are worried that some of the clinic's medicine maybe be contaminated. That way, when the press comes to interview you or Jorge Manuel, you can defend the clinic and say what great work they are doing and promise to investigate where these rumors are coming from. Then get the paper to publish an article that only says that some of the clinic's medicines were tested and found to be counterfeit Ozempic. Then you can hold a press conference, again praising the clinic and promising to get to the bottom of whoever is selling them counterfeit medicine. You need to get the public concerned and worried. But if anyone questions you, you have to always talk about how upstanding the clinic is, and how some supplier is defrauding them. Then maybe you can get a subpoena from Judge Cordela for all of the clinic's shipping and receiving records. Then you have an excuse to start interviewing all the staff. Then you can find out who controls the pharmacy inside the clinic; who decides which patients got what medicine from which box; and who distributes the medicines to the nurses to hand out to the patients. You need to find someone to flip, someone who can testify in court against this Dr. Crown. Only then will you be able to arrest him."

Don Fernando started to slump back in his chair. He looked depressed. "What if this Jim Crown goes back to the States, Dani?"

"You'd have to let him go. You need to play the long game here, don Fernando. You don't have any evidence to convict him, so there is no point to arresting him. You'd only be tipping your hand. If you can get some employee of the clinic to flip on him, then you can issue an arrest warrant for him. Until then, you have to let him operate."

Don Fernando frowned and shook his head. "I miss the old days, Dani. But I am afraid you are right. I will call my nephew at the Panama Press newspaper. He is a good boy. He will help me."

CHAPTER FIFTEEN

The next afternoon, the Panama Press carried a short article about possible counterfeit Ozempic imports into Panama by unscrupulous foreign criminals. Crown Weight-Loss Clinic was not mentioned by name. The language of the article merely carried the vague but unsettling assertion that "local clinics were concerned that their supplies had been contaminated." Jim Crown was made aware of the article by several patients who asked him directly if their medicine was safe. He reassured them that the clinic only purchased medicines from reputable pharmaceutical manufacturers, and that all of their stock was routinely tested for purity. He tried to tell himself that the article was just coincidental.

But the next day brought a new article. This time the article mentioned his clinic by name and claimed that anonymous sources had reported that his clinic was dispensing counterfeit Ozempic. The report contained an interview with Jorge Manuel, the Chief of Police of La Chorrera, who denounced the rumor-mongering and defended the reputation of the clinic and all the medical professionals in the city. Jim Crown remembered Jorge Manuel and was glad he had schmoozed him a few weeks earlier. Jim Crown got a phone call from a reporter who asked for his comments on the story. He told the reporter that his clinic was beyond reproach, that all his Ozempic came straight from the Novo Nordisk pharmaceutical company in Denmark, and that any such rumors were the work of disgruntled competitors. The reporter seemed satisfied with that quote.

However, that call was followed by several calls from his investors in New York City. They had received word of the story and wanted to know what the hell was going on. They didn't care where the rumors came from. (They certainly didn't care if the rumors were true or not.) The only thing they cared about is that the rumors existed at all. Bad rumors can tank an IPO. Jim Crown read them the quotes from Jorge Manuel from the article that defended his clinic. But the investors didn't care. They chewed his ass as if *he* had started the rumors. They warned him that they might have to shut down the IPO if he got any more bad press.

That did it, Jim Crown thought as he hung up the phone. He would have to get rid of all of what he called his 'special pharma'—all those magical substitutions that kept his profit margin so high. He had worked so hard to develop overseas contacts, to receive these illicit shipments, to mark the boxes so only he and one trusted associate knew which drugs were which. Now he had to hide them. He was thinking fast. There was no time to waste. He would move them to his condo tonight. Between now and the IPOs release, he would only use legit medicine. Shit. That was going to be expensive. He would have to doctor the books again. Once the IPO was released and the heat died down, he could move the boxes back to the clinic and make use of the drugs. But for now, he had to act.

He left his office and went out to the common area in front of the examination rooms.

"Where's Mike?" he asked one of the nurses.

"He's interviewing a patient."

"Well, tell him to come see me as soon as he's done. I'll be in my office."

A few minutes later, Michael Lynch appeared at Jim Crown's office door. He was dressed in scrubs, with a stethoscope around his neck, as if he were a doctor or nurse. In fact, he was the chief administrator of the clinic, with no medical training whatsoever.

Jim Crown gestured for Mike to come into the office and close the door.

"Mike, I need your help tonight. I'm getting too much heat from this article today. I want to move our special pharma out of here. We can use your van and take the stuff to my place tonight after we close."

"Have you heard anything from the cops?"

"No, and that's what worries me. I don't know what's going on. My lawyer says for us to simply sit tight and do nothing, but this waiting is killing me. I've gotten three calls from New York already, one from BlackRock and two from Glenn at J.P. Morgan. We need to keep a lid on everything until next Thursday. If the police come back, I want our place to be absolutely clean!"

Mike nodded. "Will do, boss. I'll pull the van around back when it gets dark, and we can load her up."

"Thanks, Mike. You're a good man."

*   *   *

But that night, things did not go exactly as Jim Crown had planned. Mike Lynch had parked his van at the clinic's back door, and he and Jim Crowned filled the van with twenty boxes of medicines. But as soon as he shut the van's door, don Fernando and several police officers pulled up in their police car, blocking the van's exit. This time, don Fernando and his officers were wearing their police uniforms.

Jim Crown immediately recognized don Fernando as the big man who had manhandled him at the first raid. He stood frozen, staring at don Fernando, not believing his own eyes. Mike Lynch, on the other hand, immediately bolted, and tried to run around the other side of the building. But a minute later, two police officers appeared, each holding the flailing Mike Lynch by the arms.

Don Fernando pointed to Mike Lynch and said to his officers, "Arrest him."

"For what!? This is our property," yelled Jim Crown.

"We have received a report of a robbery in progress," don Fernando replied calmly. "And it certainly appears to us that that is what is going on. We must investigate. We will have to seize this van and all these boxes as evidence."

"This is our property!" Jim Crown shouted again. "I'm Jim Crown, the owner of this clinic. We were simply moving some supplies."

"It appears to us that we have interrupted a burglary. I'm sure we can sort all this out after we analyze all this evidence."

"You can't do this!" Jim Crown shouted.

"Santiago," don Fernando called to one of his officers. "Write this Jim Crown a receipt for the van and all the boxes. Then he is free to go. The other man we will take into custody for questioning."

And thus it was that ten minutes later, Jim Crown was left standing alone behind the clinic, holding a paper receipt in his hand. The police were gone. The van was gone. All his special pharma medicine had been seized. And Mike Lynch had been arrested. Jim Crown felt that he was in a dream. He looked around. He was completely alone. The only sound heard was crickets chirping in the bushes.

CHAPTER SIXTEEN

Dan Landes got up late the next morning. He had spent the night before entertaining a bottle of Old Parr Whisky and woke up regretting it. He looked at the clock, shook his head, and forced himself to crawl out of bed.

He decided that he needed something to eat, although there was nothing in the fridge. So, he threw on the clothes from the day before and headed out the door. He would shower later, he thought, after he ate and felt better.

There was a small breakfast joint just two blocks away called Fonda de Linda, 'fonda' being the Panamanian slang for tiny eating place, and Linda being the owner of said breakfast shack.

Linda knew Dan well. He only came there for breakfast when he was hungover. She knew exactly what he needed to eat—he didn't need to tell her. She watched him take a seat at one of the outdoor picnic tables in the shade and then immediately brought him a cup of coffee. Then she returned to the kitchen to prepare a dish of scrambled eggs, bacon, rice and beans, and fried plantain. Everything was already prepared except for the eggs, but they only took a minute to whip up on the hot grill. By Dan's third sip of coffee, she was bringing him out a steaming plate of hangover food, for which he was very grateful.

After a few minutes, Linda returned to his table with a copy of the morning's paper that an earlier customer had left behind. She figured he might enjoy looking at it while he ate.

Dan nodded thanks, took another bite of food, and opened the paper to the front page. But when he saw the lead story, his food almost fell out of his mouth. The headline read: "Police Raid Leads to Suicide." The sub-headline read: "Clinic Owner Dead." He read the first paragraph, blinked in disbelief, and then read it again. The La Chorrera police had responded to a robbery-in-progress at the Crown Weight-Loss Clinic and discovered one of the employees moving boxes of medicine out of a back door and into a van. They arrested him, and he confessed to helping the owner of the clinic, a certain Dr. James Crown, substitute counterfeit and illegal drugs for the real medicines in the clinic's pharmacy. When the police returned to the clinic to arrest the owner, he apparently had died of a self-inflicted gunshot wound.

Dan read the article three times. He couldn't believe it. He took his cell phone out of his pocket and dialed don Fernando.

"Ah, hello Dani. Good morning, what a beautiful day," don Fernando answered.

"Don Fernando, what the hell happened last night?"

"Last night? Oh yes, *that*. What a terrible thing, Dani," don Fernando said with an almost airy tone to his voice. "An absolute tragedy," he added.

"What happened?!" Dan demanded again.

Don Fernando laughed. "Well," he explained, "it's a long story. But the short version—strictly between you and me, Dani—is that we had been keeping surveillance on the clinic. Last night, we saw this Dr. Crown and one of his flunkies moving boxes out of the back door of the clinic after the clinic had closed. I had figured they might do this— that's why I was keeping an eye on them. So, I arrested the flunky—is that how you say it? Flunky? I like that word. You gringos have such great words. Anyway, I arrested the flunky and took him down to the station and had a little talk with him. He confessed to the whole deal. Meanwhile, Koki drove the boxes of medicine over to Dr. Vargas. I really had to twist her arm to open the laboratory so late in the evening. But she is such a sweet person, she did it for me. She tested the medicine, and they all turned out to be bad drugs. But when

Koki went back to the clinic to arrest Dr. Crown, he had shot himself. A tragic end, don't you think?"

Dan's brain was spinning. "I can't believe this, don Fernando. This is just mind-boggling!"

"I don't know what that word means, Dani, but to be honest, I am very pleased with the results. We have shut down that clinic."

Dan was just shaking his head, holding onto his cell phone. But his detective brain was clicking on, despite his hangover. He started to ask don Fernando some questions.

"How long have you been watching the clinic?"

"Ever since the first raid, Dani. I figured that they would eventually try to hide the bad drugs, especially once the newspaper articles started coming out. I really want to thank you for that idea, Dani. It was brilliant. You are so smart."

"And, well, wait… so you were watching the clinic," Dan sputtered, "and last night you saw what?"

"As I told you, Dani, Doctor Crown and one of his flunkies were moving boxes into a van. We waited until they were ready to leave and then we jumped out of the bushes. You should have seen their faces!" Don Fernando laughed. "The little one tried to run, but we caught him. The Doctor Crown was screaming like a little girl. It was great. We arrested the flunky and took him to Villa Rosario where I had a little talk with him."

Dan knew what don Fernando's little talks entailed. "And he confessed?"

"Oh, he sang like a bird. But we had to wait until Dr. Vargas tested the medicines. Once they came back positive for bad drugs, she called me and told me. Then I called Koki and told him to go back to the clinic and arrest the good doctor. Unfortunately, he had killed himself by the time Koki arrived. Put the gun under his chin and blew off the top of his head. Very unfortunate."

"I'm stunned, don Fernando. I'm just stunned."

"Yes, we are treating the whole clinic as a crime scene. My men are guarding it now. It will not reopen."

Dan frowned. It still didn't make total sense to him.

"Don Fernando," he asked, "how did you arrest that one guy? I mean, *why* did you only arrest the one guy, and on what grounds did you arrest him?"

"Simple, Dani. I only needed one employee to confess, and he looked like the confessing type."

"And what did you arrest him for?"

"Suspicion of burglary, Dani."

"But, it was their own clinic, don Fernando. They were on their own property, moving their own boxes."

"Yes, I know, Dani. But it looked like a burglary, so that was good enough. And now that the little one has confessed and the doctor is dead, no one can deny that there was a crime going on. It is a good result, Dani. Life will go on. Koki's job is protected. The city council cannot fire him for closing down a clinic when the owner had committed suicide because he got caught with illegal drugs. La Chorrera will lose some tourism, it's true. But the city will survive."

Dan was quiet. He knew he would think more clearly when his hangover was gone. But for now, the news seemed so crazy to him.

"Okay, don Fernando, listen. I'm going to come over and talk with you tomorrow, okay? I need some time to absorb this. But tomorrow, I'll come over and we can talk."

"Any time, Dani," don Fernando said warmly. "It's always good to see you."

CHAPTER SEVENTEEN

By the next morning, Dan was feeling better. And he had many questions. He called don Fernando and asked if he could come by the police station around noon, just to chat. Don Fernando said that would be splendid. He seemed to be in a good mood.

Dan wasn't the only one who had questions. That morning also saw an unusual number of private jets land at the Panama City airport, along with the regularly scheduled airline flights. A host of lawyers, accountants, and insurance claims agents had been hastily ordered to Panama by J.P. Morgan, Merrill Lynch, two insurance companies, and several hedge funds. They swarmed into La Chorrera like angry ants in black suits, all trying to defend their nest—or in this case, their nest egg—that had been damaged.

But don Fernando had carefully prepped Jorge Manuel and given him an unassailable story to present to any annoying lawyers: Panama had been victimized by an influx of counterfeit weight-loss drugs; Jorge Manuel could point to the newspaper articles that detailed that fact. There had been rumors of counterfeit drugs at the Crown Weight-Loss Clinic; but Jorge Manuel was again able to point to the newspaper articles, where he had denounced these rumors and defended the clinic. However, because of public health concerns, a judge had issued a search warrant to seize samples of the clinic's drugs for testing. This was done as discretely as possible, to prevent negative publicity for the clinic. Unfortunately, the rumors turned out to be true. But the police continued their investigation, again without alerting the press, in an effort to preserve the clinic's due process rights. When the police received a report of a burglary at the clinic, they rushed to the scene, to find one of the employees loading up a van in the back of the clinic. They arrested the employee, and he made a surprising confession which led to the testing of more of the clinic's medicines, which turned out to contain counterfeit semaglutide product, amphetamines, and mislabeled insulin. The owner, the late Dr. James Crown, must have seen the writing on the wall, because he shot himself to avoid the public humiliation of being arrested and convicted of a massive fraud.

It was a good story, and Jorge Manuel felt confident he could handle the onslaught of gringo lawyers that don Fernando predicted would show up. The most important thing, don Fernando explained to his nephew, was to never appear ruffled or caught off guard by a lawyer's question. If a lawyer asks a question you can't answer, don Fernando explained, always say that the investigation is ongoing, and you just can't comment on it until the inquiry is complete.

As don Fernando had predicted, Jorge Manuel received many calls that morning. Everybody wanted to meet with him. Don Fernando had advised him to schedule a question-and-answer session that afternoon rather than to make individual appointments. "It will save time," don Fernando had said, "and questions are actually easier to deflect in a public meeting than in a private conversation."

So, Jorge Manuel scheduled a conference that afternoon at one-thirty to meet with the lawyers, accountants, and others who had so suddenly appeared in his little town. He called don Fernando and asked his uncle to come to the meeting, just for moral support. Don Fernando agreed.

At noon, Dan appeared at don Fernando's office door.

"Ah, Dani. Come in. You are just in time. I made a fresh pot of coffee. I have to go over to La Chorrera in forty minutes or so. Koki is having his first press conference." Don Fernando laughed. "I want to see how he does. Maybe you can come with me."

"Is this conference related to the death of Jim Crown?" Dan asked as he helped himself to coffee.

"Yes, of course," responded don Fernando. "It's big news. Rich gringo shoots himself because he got caught trying to poison his clients. La Chorrera hasn't had this much gossip since that Canadian gringo got caught with two wives last year. Both wives almost beat him to death, but the court acquitted them! Ha. I understand the two women are best friends now."

"Yes, I remember that," Dan said. "But back to the Crown clinic: Who discovered the body of Jim Crown?"

"Koki and his men. Koki had taken the boxes of medicine to Dr. Vargas. She called me to tell me the drugs were all either counterfeit or illegal. I had her put Koki on the line and told him to go straight to the clinic and arrest that evil doctor. But when he got there, he found the doctor dead on the clinic floor. It was a mess. Then he called me. and I went over to help him secure the scene."

"I see. Let me ask you this, don Fernando: why didn't you arrest Dr. Crown when you arrested that other guy?"

"There was no need to, Dani. I had enough probable cause to seize the drugs, and I wanted to arrest the flunky. I knew I could make *him* talk. And I was pretty sure the boxes of medicine would turn out to be dirty, because... well, why else would they be moving them at night? So, when the flunky confessed, then I had enough evidence to arrest Dr. Crown. It was perfect."

Dan nodded. It *was* perfect. "So, let me get the sequence straight, don Fernando. You watched Dr. Crown and his employee loading up a van with drugs last night. You seized the drugs and arrested the employee. Jorge Manuel took the drugs to Panama City while you interrogated the employee. Dr. Vargas calls you with the lab results, and then you tell Jorge Manuel to drive to the clinic and arrest Dr. Crown. Is that how it went down?"

Don Fernando nodded.

How did you know that Dr. Crown would still be at the clinic?"

Don Fernando paused, frowned, then said, "It was just a hunch, Dani. I figured he would be there straightening up the place, maybe trying to think of an alibi."

"And who is this guy you arrested?" Dan asked.

"I do not remember his name, Dani. He was just an employee there. But he knew all about the crime. So, I think he worked for Dr. Crown for a long time."

"Is he still in your jail?"

"Yes, Dani. He had a rough night."

"And what will happen to him?"

Don Fernando paused again and appeared to be thinking. "Well, I don't know. I guess I will just release him in a few days. I don't need him anymore."

"You're not going to charge him with anything?"

"Well, Dani, I can't charge him with burglary or stealing. He was just doing what his boss told him to do. And, in fact, the boxes did belong to the clinic. I suppose I could charge him with conspiracy and fraud, but you know how it is. Those crimes are so hard to prove here. I would be tied up in court for years. I will notify Immigration. They will deport him when I release him. He will never come back to Panama again. Problem solved."

Dan thought about how the Panamanian justice system was both primitive and efficient. What don Fernando had said was true. The Panamanian authorities simply did not have the resources, personnel, or training to prosecute complex white-collar crime. They could barely prosecute simple money laundering. If this guy—whatever his name was—was deported, he would no longer be Panama's problem. And the Feds could decide if they wanted to prosecute him.

"And the clinic?" Dan asked. "What will happen to it?"

"It is closed," don Fernando said. "We have officers guarding it. We have to do our follow-up investigation, and that will take a while. I told the officers to take their time. I hope the clinic will stay closed. What they were doing was so wrong."

"Well, it affected you personally," Dan said.

"Yes, Dani. I had to hire a company to come in and repair all the damage I did to my kitchen. It cost me a lot of money. I was not happy."

Dan nodded. "And how's Ana Luisa doing? You had said she was so excited about going to the Crown clinic, but she only got to go that one time."

"She's doing well, actually. She's joined a gym and is working out. Speaking of that, her father Judge Andrés Cordela called me this morning. He was so mad at me last week for using his daughter to get him to give me that search warrant. Ha! I thought he was never going to talk to me again. But he called me this morning to thank me for, as he put it 'getting the job done without tarnishing his office's reputation.' Ha, he's just like all judges: he's fine as long as he's not in trouble. He ended up appearing virtuous for giving me a search warrant to close down a fraud, so he's happy. The way things turned out, the politicians in Panama can't blame him for doing the right thing."

Don nodded his head. He was thinking.

"Yes, things kind of turned out well," Dan said.

"Finish your coffee, Dani, and come with me to La Chorrera. We can go watch Koki's first press conference and then take him out to lunch to celebrate."

CHAPTER EIGHTEEN

Jorge Manuel's question-and-answer session went reasonably well. He started off by reciting the story that don Fernando had given him, and then opened up the floor for questions. To Jorge Manuel's innocent ears, all the questions seemed selfish and demanding. The lawyers wanted to know which court had jurisdiction over the clinic so they could file pleadings to take control of the building and its operations; the accountants wanted to know when they could get access to the clinic's books to do audits; and the insurance claims agents wanted to know about Panama's liability laws. None of the questioners seemed concerned with the twenty local nurses and staff who suddenly found themselves without jobs. And certainly none of the questions expressed any concern that so many patients had been exposed to dangerous drugs. In fact, Jorge Manuel noticed that many in the audience seemed pleased when he mentioned that Panama's liability laws—such as they are—would make it difficult for patients to sue the clinic.

Don Fernando and Dan stood off to the side of the gaggle of suits. Dan noticed that don Fernando was watching the crowd very carefully. At one point, don Fernando leaned over to Dan and whispered, "Do you see that short fat man over there, the one with the wire-rimmed glasses?

"Yeah," said Dan. "What about him?"

"I do not trust him, Dani. He gives off—how do you say?—a bad vibe."

Dan watched the man for a little bit. To Dan's eyes, he didn't appear any different than any of the other twenty white men in suits standing in the room, although Dan did notice one peculiar thing about him: Instead of asking questions, he would whisper to a young man standing beside him, and the younger man would raise his hand and ask the question. Dan thought that was odd. But he didn't notice any particular vibe about the man, one way or another. Dan did notice that the younger man was the only one who asked a question about the late Dr. Jim Crown. The young man wanted to know at what morgue the body was being stored.

The short fat man in question was, in fact, a certain C.N. Jones. No one knew what his initials stood for—he refused to tell anyone. He had a mistress back in New York who called him by his initials, but even she didn't know what they stood for. Everyone else simply referred to him as Mr. Jones. Even his driver's license only carried his initials. Mr. Jones was not a lawyer; he wasn't an insurance claims agent. He was, in fact, an investment banker for J.P. Morgan. It was fitting that a man with only initials for a first name worked for a bank that only had initials for a first name.

Mr. Jones was not happy to be in Panama. The heat was unbearable to him. But his department back at J.P. Morgan had a lot of money invested in Crown Weight-Loss Incorporated, and Mr. Jones had flown all the way to Panama that morning with just one goal in mind: to get the Crown Weight-Loss Clinic up and running as soon as possible.

As Jorge Manuel was finishing up the last few questions, don Fernando kept his eye on Mr. Jones. Don Fernando had a certain instinct about people. Thirty plus years of being a police chief had honed his intuition about criminals. To him, criminals had a certain vibe, almost like a smell, which made the hairs on the back of his neck stand up and caused him to squint his eyes and stare. He watched as the young associate of Mr. Jones approached Jorge Manuel as he was stepping away from the podium. The young man spoke briefly with Jorge Manuel and then brought him over to Mr. Jones. The young man was clearly introducing Mr. Jones to Jorge Manuel. They shook hands, and Mr. Jones offered his business card to Jorge Manuel, who accepted it, looked at it, and then placed it in his shirt pocket. The two men talked for a moment. Then Jorge Manuel shook Mr. Jones's hand again and went to chat with one of his officers. Don Fernando watched Mr. Jones give some instructions to his young associate, who nodded his head and then left the room quickly. Mr. Jones also left the room, but at a much more relaxed pace.

Don Fernando caught Jorge Manuel's eye and gestured for him to come over to where he and Dan were standing.

"Who was that gringo, Koki?" don Fernando asked.

"I never met him before uncle. But he gave me his card."

"Let me see it, Koki."

Jorge Manuel handed don Fernando the business card.

"C.N. Jones, Vice-President of Acquisitions, J.P. Morgan," don Fernando read aloud. "What does this mean, Dani, this *Acquisitions*?"

"It's when one company buys up enough stock in another company to be able to control it."

"Is it a good thing?" don Fernando asked.

"No, not really," said Dan. "It can make whoever sells the stock rich, but it's rarely a good thing for the company. Businesses buy other companies to make money, not to make the company any better. And this guy works for J.P. Morgan. That's an investment bank. They *only* buy businesses to make money."

"Hmmph," grunted don Fernando. "Gringos—they are only interested in money. What did he want, Koki?"

"He just complimented me on handling the meeting. Then he asked me who was the judge who issued the search warrant for clinic."

Don Fernando grunted again. "And you told him it was Andrés Cordela?"

"Sí, uncle. It's no secret. It was in the newspapers."

"True," said don Fernando. "Listen, Koki. Keep your eye on that guy. If he contacts you again, or if you even see him around the clinic, let me know."

"Of course, uncle. Do you think he is a *ladrón*?" Jorge Manuel asked, using the Spanish word for thief.

"Sí, Koki. I think he is the worst kind, the kind that wears a suit."

CHAPTER NINETEEN

Don Fernando's suspicions about Mr. Jones were correct. Besides his young assistant, Mr. Jones had brought three lawyers with him to Panama. They got to work right away, filing motions in Judge Cordela's courtroom to be declared executors of Dr. Crown's clinic. Given the documents that Mr. Jones's lawyers provided (showing that Mr. Jones owned sixty percent of the stock of Crown Weight-Loss Incorporated), Judge Cordela had no choice but to grant Mr. Jones's request. As the new owner of the Crown Clinic, Mr. Jones put his lawyers to work, sending them to visit legislators in Panama City, to explain their new-found desire to help the economy of Panama by reopening the clinic. Of course, while the lawyers were visiting the legislators, they made generous contributions to the reelection funds of said legislators. The lawyers explained that it would be very helpful for all concerned for the police investigation to be quickly concluded, and the clinic allowed to reopen.

Don Fernando found out about all this through a series of phone calls, including one from Jorge Manuel.

"Uncle, remember you told me to let you know if that Mr. Jones tried to contact me? Well, he called me today. He wants to meet with me tomorrow. He says he's bringing his team and wants to discuss the clinic. I also got a call from the office of the Ministry of the Judiciary, asking when I am going to wrap up this clinic investigation."

"I am not surprised, Koki," don Fernando said. "I got a call today as well, from Andrés Cordela. It turns out that this Mr. Jones is the new owner of the Crown Weight-Loss Clinic. Andrés told me that he has been making the rounds at the National Assembly, paying friendly visits to many legislators—and I do mean *paying*, if you get my meaning."

"What should I do, uncle?"

"Well, Koki, it is always difficult to confront this type of corruption head-on. Are you done with interviewing all the ex-employees?"

"Oh, yes, uncle. A few days ago. And we did not uncover anything new. I was just keeping the clinic closed because you asked me to."

"Well, yes... that was my original hope. But we must adapt to new circumstances. We need to find out the intentions of this Mr. Jones. Go ahead and set up a meeting with him, as he requested. I will come to help you, and I will bring Dani. We need to walk a fine line with this gringo Jones. He needs to think we are his friend, that we are trying to help him navigate the difficult bureaucracy of Panama. Speaking of bureaucracy, have you ordered an autopsy of the body of that Dr. Crown? That might buy us some more time."

"I could not do that, uncle."

"Why not, Koki?"

"Because that Mr. Jones already took the body for a private autopsy."

"Really?"

"Yes, uncle, he showed up at the morgue the day after my question-and-answer conference with a court order. Evidently, he has power-of-attorney from some next-of-kin."

"Interesting," said don Fernando. "I wonder why he wanted an autopsy. It was obviously a suicide. Hmm. We must not underestimate this man, Koki. Go ahead and set up that meeting for tomorrow and let me know what time it will be. Dani and I will be there."

*　　　*　　　*

The next afternoon at two o'clock, eight people gathered at a table in the conference room in the La Chorrera police department. On one side of the table was Jorge Manuel, don Fernando, and a very reluctant Dan Landes, whom don Fernando had dragged along to the meeting. On the other side of the table sat Mr. Jones, his assistant, and his three attorneys.

The session got off to a tense start. Jorge Manuel had opened the meeting by introducing don Fernando as the person leading the investigation into the substitution of counterfeit and illicit drugs at the clinic. Then he introduced Dan Landes as simply a friend of the police force, who was only there to help with any language translation issues.

"Oh," said Mr. Jones. "My assistant speaks excellent Spanish. I'm sure we won't need Mr. Landes's services."

Dan did not want to be at the meeting in the first place, but Mr. Jones's condescending tone annoyed him. But before Dan could say anything, don Fernando spoke up:

"Oh no, no, gentlemen. Mr. Landes is not here to translate Spanish. He is more of—how would you say it?—a *cultural* translator. We Panamanians have found out over the years—found out the hard way—that English is a difficult language, not for what is being said, but for what is *not* being said. It is hard to get at the true meaning of things when different cultures are involved, don't you agree? Mr. Landes is good at helping us to *connect the dots*, to use an expression."

Dan noticed that don Fernando was using his most friendly smile and his most ingratiating voice while at the same time asserting Dan's right to be at the meeting.

"Very well," said Mr. Jones. "Well, I'll get straight to the point. We'd like to know when we can get our clinic back. As you know, the court in Panama City granted us executor status over the clinic. J.P. Morgan financed the upcoming IPO of Crown Weight-Loss Incorporated and currently owns the majority of stock in the corporation. Provisions in the stock acquisition contract provided that control of the clinic would transfer to J.P. Morgan upon the death or incapacity of the CEO, the late James Crown. Originally, we had anticipated an initial public offering this month. But because of the unfortunate death of the CEO, we've had to push that IPO back two months.

"This clinic is the flagship of the corporation. We are very anxious to get it afloat. We have five other clinics currently under construction in other countries. Most of them are bigger than this clinic. But it is this clinic that is currently in the public eye and represents the health benefits that Crown Weight-Loss Incorporated can provide. As such, we would like to get access to the clinic and get it back into operation. Clients have made reservations months in advance to come here to avail themselves of our weight-loss products. Right now, you've got officers guarding the building and not allowing us in. We'd like to get our building back."

Don Fernando was still smiling and nodding his head in apparent agreement. To Dan, it seemed unnatural to see don Fernando smile this much.

"Understandable, señor, very understandable," don Fernando said. "But there is this small matter of the fraud that was going on inside the clinic. You know... the substitution of counterfeit drugs, and even street drugs that were being substituted for your very fine weight-loss medicines. The amount of illicit drugs that we seized was rather large. This is an issue that affects public health."

"Yes," said Mr. Jones, "but there is no evidence that any of the drugs that were found ever made their way into the prescriptions of any of the clinic's patients. Our theory is that this associate of Dr. Crown, this Michael Lynch, was attempting to run his own drug-dealing business from inside the clinic. We believe that Dr. Crown discovered this crime, and that he made the ill-advised decision to get rid of this bad apple rather than call the police. He didn't want to tarnish the name of the clinic. That was the wrong decision, clearly. And it backfired on him and caused him to take his own life. But what these unfortunate events have highlighted is the need for the clinic to have stricter controls over the supply and administration of our medicines. Our new leadership team is dedicated to making sure that our patients only get the legitimate semaglutide products that they need. We have an entirely new prescription control system that we are eager to put into place."

Don Fernando was still smiling and nodding his head as he spoke: "Yes, yes. Well, I'm not sure I can agree with everything you said. First of all, we *do* have evidence that the illegal drugs made it into patient prescriptions. We have actual samples taken from actual patients that tested positive for amphetamine. Second, we do have evidence that one patient died as a result of this substitution."

Dan noticed a tiny bit of color drain from Mr. Jones's face. Clearly, this was new information to him. "I… I haven't heard anything about this," he sputtered.

Don Fernando gave a small shrug. "Well, Mr. Jones, the investigation is still ongoing. This information has not been made public. We haven't released these details, because we don't want to do anything that would damage the fine reputation of the clinic."

The lawyer sitting next to Mr. Jones leaned over and whispered something into Mr. Jones's ear. Mr. Jones nodded and seemed to be thinking.

Mr. Jones leaned forward and said, "Our plan is to rehire all of the existing local staff when we reopen. In fact, our plan is to hire more local staff."

"Yes, that would be good thing. Unemployment is a problem in La Chorrera. I'm sure those people would be very happy to get their jobs back."

"And, of course, there is the benefit to the local economy that the tourists would bring," said Mr. Jones.

"Yes, a tremendous boom," agreed don Fernando.

"But we wouldn't be able to do that if we had to close the clinic due to bad publicity."

"No, no, your hands would be tied," said don Fernando. "And it would a great loss to La Chorrera."

Mr. Jones leaned back in his chair and said, "So, we understand each other."

"Yes," said don Fernando, "and you can see why we need a few more weeks to complete our investigation."

"Yes, of course," said Mr. Jones. "Can you provide me with the name of the patient who died?"

"No," said don Fernando and smiled. "Not until we our investigation is complete."

"What about an advanced copy of the final report?" asked Mr. Jones. "Could you give us that?"

"Well, you know, Panama is a strange country, Mr. Jones. Some reports are final reports, and some are not. What would be helpful to us, what would speed up the investigation, is if we could operate in peace—if we could complete our investigation without being distracted by outside pressures."

Mr. Jones nodded his head. "I understand what you mean," he said.

And with that, Mr. Jones signaled to his entourage, and they all stood up and left the room.

After Mr. Jones and his group were gone, don Fernando's smile disappeared. He turned to Dan and said, "I told you I did not like that guy."

"You handled him well," Dan replied.

"Ah, all I accomplished was to gain maybe two weeks. I'm not sure where that gets me, Dani."

"What about the investigation?" Dan asked.

"It's very frustrating," don Fernando said with a frown. "We've looked through all their patient medical records, looking for their file on the woman that died, this Laura Jenkins. But it's not there. They must have removed her file and destroyed it. Koki has interviewed all the ex-employees, but no one remembers a Laura Jenkins in particular."

"Are you still holding that employee Michael Lynch in your jail?" Dan asked.

"Yes. I was going to let him go, but then I decided he might be useful. I was hoping he might remember Laura Jenkins, but he does not. There were so many patients where they were substituting medicines."

"But uncle, you have such a great case. So many witnesses! You have this employee who can testify how the clinic was switching medicines; you have amphetamines they gave you and the amphetamines they gave Enrique Calvino;

you have the insulin shot they gave to Ana Luisa, and you have the dead woman with amphetamines in her system."

"Well," said Dan, "I'm not so sure it's an airtight case. So much of the evidence is circumstantial. We can't prove that the clinic gave Laura Jenkins amphetamines. And the fact that Ana Luisa had elevated insulin in her body and no Ozempic is not proof that the clinic gave her the insulin. It's good circumstantial evidence, but it's not direct proof…"

"I cannot use Ana Luisa," interrupted don Fernando. Andrés Cordela told me in no uncertain terms to keep her out of any trial. And I cannot go against Andrés—he is my brother-in-law."

"But you still have the amphetamines that the clinic gave you and Enrique Calvino," exclaimed Jorge Manuel. "That plus the testimony of that employee would be enough to convict the clinic."

"No," said don Fernando. "It would only be enough to convict the dead doctor and his flunky. There is no evidence that anyone else in the clinic knew what was going on. Dr. Crown kept tight control over the pharmacy. I have interviewed this flunky several times. Other people in the clinic might have thought that the doctor's complete control of the pharmacy was extreme, but I am convinced that only the doctor and the flunky knew what was going on."

Don Fernando noticed that both his nephew and Dan were giving him a quizzical look. "You don't understand," he said. "I am not interested in convicting this flunky. He is just a pawn. I can have him deported. And the doctor is dead. What I want is to close the clinic down permanently. I don't want it ever to open again."

"I don't think that's possible, don Fernando," Dan said softly. "In the United States, you can prosecute a corporation for a crime. But not here in Panama. You can only go after the individuals who commit a crime."

"I know," said don Fernando and shook his head back and forth slowly. "But I would like to find a way."

"There is a lot of money behind this company, don

Fernando," Dan said. "Look how many lawyers showed up. I don't see how you can stop them from reopening the clinic. Besides, maybe after this scandal, they might put in safety controls to prevent the contamination of medicine."

Don Fernando just shook his head. "If it's one thing I know, Dani, it's that people always repeat their behavior. And corporations are no different. If this clinic tried to make money by using fake medicine once, they will do it again."

CHAPTER TWENTY

Don Fernando's opinion about corporations repeating their crimes was not unfounded. But the fact is, corporations—like people—are also subject to external forces. The week after the meeting at the La Chorrera Police Department, Mr. Jones was on the phone with one of those external forces, namely his boss in New York City.

"Let me give you the update, Glenn," Mr. Jones was saying. "The cops finally gave me all the accounting files and patient records for the clinic, and my lawyers have gone over them with a fine-tooth comb. It looks like Jim was definitely cooking the books, but he wasn't doing it to fabricate the clinic's profitability. He was only doing it to hide all the speed, insulin juice, and knockoff semaglutide he was importing and passing off as Ozempic. We set up a program to calculate what his bottom line would have been these last few months if he hadn't been swapping drugs, and the figures are still pretty good. This clinic is a viable business, Glenn. It may not be a rocket IPO, but it's a solid launch. I don't think you should push the IPO back any further…

"… No, no, Glenn. I'm confident about this. I think I can get the go-ahead from these yahoo cops to reopen the clinic next week. We've contacted all the former employees, and they are anxious to return. I've also contacted all the clients on the waiting list, and we've got an 85% positive response. I think that once we reopen, we can be at full capacity within a week…

"… Yes, yes, I understand, Glenn, I understand. But here's the issue: if you want to hit the original IPO goals, I can do that. I can make that happen. We found that encrypted file on Jim's computer, and we were able to decode it. It has all his suppliers for synthetic semaglutide: names, websites, emails, prices, you name it. Now, he went too far, I agree. He should never have used speed and insulin. That was just fucking stupid. But his sources for synthetic semaglutide are solid…

"… What's that? Well, yes, I know… I've seen the articles, too. Well, my office has been cranking out counter-position pieces, claiming this Mike Lynch guy was using his position at the clinic to run his own clandestine operation. We leaked photos of his invoices, showing how he used his position at the clinic to order amphetamine from Mexico. And we're maintaining our position that no patients were ever exposed to that crap. In fact, Jim's suicide kind of helps us. Make him look like he was so disgraced to discover Mike's betrayal of his dream…"

"… What? Well, whatever you want, Glenn. I'm just saying I can get synthetic semaglutide at the drop of a hat… Yes, I understand… What? No, I haven't seen that article... They said what?... Wow... Okay, well, we can play it 100% clean for the IPO, Glenn. But I don't want to give up Jim's business model, Glenn. Walmart and Costco didn't make their nut by selling only name-brand merchandise, Glenn. At some point, we've got to switch to a house brand… Yeah, yeah, okay, *once* we establish public trust... Yes, exactly. Then we'll have exit liquidity… Right, okay… I'm going to forward that encrypted file to you. Take a look at it. Jim certainly did his homework on that…

"… Okay, good, Glenn. I'll give you another call in a few days. I need to pay another visit to these stupid cops. But I should have a date certain for the clinic reopening in a few days… Yes, good… Alright, bye."

Mr. Jones hung up the phone. Damn that Jim Crown, he thought to himself. We had the perfect business model, and he had to fuck it up by using speed and insulin. Why couldn't he have just stuck with synthetic semaglutide? We could have been billionaires. But Glenn was right. Run the business clean for another month, release the IPO, but hang onto the stock. Then we can slide the synthetic stuff back in and show a huge second quarter profit. *Then* we'll dump the stock. We can still make millions.

* * *

118

At the same moment that Mr. Jones was calculating his potential profit, don Fernando was talking to Dan in his office.

"I'm not sure I can keep the clinic locked up much longer, Dani. We're getting a lot of pressure from all sides. The city council of La Chorrera is calling Koki every day. The *diputados* in Panama City are calling me. I even had one hint that he could arrange a legislative position for me, if I would let the clinic reopen. Can you imagine? *Representative* Fernando? What a joke. It is very frustrating to be a police chief, Dani. Everyone wants you to arrest the small criminal, but they complain when you go after the big criminal…"

"I know it's tough, amigo," said Dan. "What do you think you're going to do?"

Dan Fernando shook his head. "I am hoping God will show me a way. I had a long heart-to-heart talk with Andrés yesterday. I went over all the evidence: how Enrique Calvino and I went in separately and were given amphetamine; how good our chain of custody was; how thorough Dr. Vargas's lab results were; and how that Michael Lynch is cooperating fully with us… and Andrés agrees it is good evidence, but he says I will never get a conviction with it, not here in Panama. The *diputados* control the judges, and money controls the *diputados*. *Qué chorizo,* Dani. Our system is completely corrupt."

Dan nodded his head.

"And worse, Dani," don Fernando continued, "is that Andrés says the *diputados* will find a way to remove me from this job if I don't get the clinic reopened. Who will protect Villa Rosario from criminals then, Dani?"

Dan shrugged. Don Fernando had been the police chief of Villa Rosario for as long as anyone could remember. It was his reputation that made many criminals think twice about doing anything in that sleepy town.

"Politics suck, don Fernando," was all Dan could think to say.

"That is true, Dani. Andrés says I should go to Mass and pray to God for a solution to this problem. I think he is right, Dani. The Church has Mass tomorrow night. I will go to Mass and pray."

But the next afternoon, before don Fernando could get to church, Mr. Jones made a surprise visit to his office.

"Ah, Police Chief Fernando," said Mr. Jones as he settled into the chair across from don Fernando's desk, "I was in the neighborhood, and took a chance that you might be in your office. Thank you so much for seeing me."

"My pleasure, Mr. Jones. It is always good to see investors in our sister city of La Chorrera. How can I be of service?"

"Well, your name came to my attention this morning," said Mr. Jones. "As you know, the La Chorrera Police Department gave us back the patient medical records for the clinic. My staff was looking through those records, trying to identify which clients might come back to the clinic when we reopen. And we happened to find your name. I did not realize that *you* had been a patient at the clinic."

Don Fernando nodded his head. "For a brief time, yes, I was."

"And how was your experience at the clinic?"

"Oh, it was very good, Mr. Jones. Yes, I would say, it was very good. I was very satisfied with it."

"And I couldn't help but notice that you were receiving the Rybelsus tablets."

"Yes," don Fernando said slowly. "That is true."

"And I remembered that you had mentioned at our meeting in La Chorrera that you had evidence that some of the clinic's patients had received amphetamines, and— if you'll pardon me for being so indiscreet—but I was wondering if perhaps you thought that... *you* might have... somehow... received amphetamines instead of Rybelsus?"

"Well, I certainly would hope that wasn't the case, Mr. Jones."

"No, of course not, I would hope that wasn't the case either. In the United States, of course, this would be what we call an *actionable* event. That is, a person who received the wrong medication could sue a pharmacy for negligence. In fact, even if they had received the right medicine but were afraid they had received the wrong medicine, they could sue for negligent infliction of emotional damage."

"We do not have those kinds of laws down here, Mr. Jones," don Fernando said.

"So, I understand. A pity, really. Negligence is such a horrible thing."

"Yes, it is," don Fernando agreed.

"Yes, it is," echoed Mr. Jones. "But that is not the reason for my visit. The reason for my visit is that we finally got a copy of the autopsy results for the late Dr. Crown."

"Oh?" said don Fernando. "Yes, I was informed you had taken possession of the body. Did you have an autopsy done?"

"Yes, by a private doctor."

"Really? How very thorough of you," said don Fernando. "And where is the body now?"

"It was cremated after the autopsy."

"I see," said don Fernando.

"It took a while for them to complete the report," said Mr. Jones. "I just received it this morning."

Don Fernando waited.

"It said he died of self-inflicted gunshot wound."

Don Fernando nodded and said, "Yes, that is how it appeared to us."

"But I thought I should give you a copy of the report," said Mr. Jones, "to help complete the paperwork on your investigation."

"Ah, yes. Very thoughtful of you," don Fernando said.

Mr. Jones pulled a folded report from the inside breast pocket of his suit jacket and placed it on don Fernando's desk.

"Well," said Mr. Jones, "I won't detain you any longer. As I said, I was just in the neighborhood and thought I would drop off that report. I'm really hoping we can get access to the clinic next week and get it opened once again."

"Yes, we will let you know."

And with that, Mr. Jones gave a quick smile, stood up and left don Fernando's office.

What an evil man, don Fernando thought as he watched him leave. He sat there for a full minute, just thinking about everything that had been said—and more importantly, everything that was unsaid—during that meeting. Then he picked up the autopsy report and read it.

Unlike most police autopsy reports, this one did not make any conclusions as to cause of death. It simply reported on the state of the body, the bullet hole in the head, the manner of death, a blood toxicology report which showed a small amount of amphetamines in the doctor's body. That was interesting, don Fernando thought, so the good doctor was a user of amphetamines. It was always careless for a dealer to use his own product.

But it wasn't until he got to the end of the second page that it became clear why Mr. Jones had given him the report. Whoever had done the autopsy had done a gunpowder residue swab of Jim Crown's hands. And it had come up negative.

Don Fernando put the report down and thought again what an evil man Mr. Jones was. That was why he had given him the report.

Don Fernando sat and thought for a long while. Then he looked at his watch. He still had two hours before Mass started. Surely God would answer his prayers.

CHAPTER TWENTY-TWO

La Chorrera was not a big city. Panama City is almost ten times the size of La Chorrera. And because of its smaller size, La Chorrera does not have the type of violent crime that occurs in bigger cities like Panama City or Colón. That's not to say that crime doesn't happen in La Chorrera. It does, but it is usually petty crime, property crime, an occasional burglary, and every once in a while, maybe an armed robbery.

That's why it was such a shock when, two days after his meeting with don Fernando, Mr. Jones turned up dead.

A passerby saw his body slumped over in the driver's seat of a rented car that was parked in front of the clinic. He had been shot once in the head. His wallet was missing. It was clearly a murder, committed during the course of a robbery, and the newspapers reported it as such. There were no witnesses. The police had no leads. Eventually, the police surmised that it was out-of-town hoodlums from Panama City who had ventured into La Chorrera looking for someone to rob. And Mr. Jones made an attractive target in his expensive suit and rental car. He just happened to be in the wrong place at the wrong time.

The lawyers for the late Mr. Jones all scrambled to figure out what to do next. But they were like ants without a queen. Frantic calls were made. Someone had to take charge. The IPO was pushed back another month. A week went by, and then one day a certain Glenn Richardson appeared in La Chorrera.

Glenn Richardson, as you may have guessed, had been Mr. Jones's boss, and Jim Crown's boss before him. He was very pissed about losing two of his employees in such a short period of time. He didn't particularly care for either of the two men, but now he had to fly down to Panama and fix their mess. Glenn Richardson was one of those corporate executives who was always pissed about something. He was all business. He never smiled. He didn't talk much. When he did, he was usually yelling. His staff back in New York kept expecting him to suffer a stroke. (Actually, they rather hoped he *would* stroke out.) But he kept on living, and he kept on making money for J.P. Morgan. So, he kept getting promotions, and new projects.

When the lawyers for the late Mr. Jones called Glenn Richardson with news of the murder, they wanted to give him all the details about what had happened. But he interrupted them and told them to simply arrange an appointment with whomever he needed to talk to in order to get the clinic reopened. Then he buzzed his secretary and told her to arrange a private jet to Panama City for the next morning. He also told her to arrange for a certain Dr. Carlson to join him on the flight.

Glenn Richardson had previously selected Dr. Carlson to take Jim Crown's place. Dr. Carlson was qualified. He had successfully managed clinics before. More importantly, he was young, and eager to please. Glenn Richardson told his secretary to tell Dr. Carlson that the timetable had been moved up, and that if he wanted the job, he'd better be on that flight the next morning.

At the airport, a private driver met the two men and drove them straight to La Chorrera. Mr. Jones's lawyers had arranged a meeting at the La Chorrera Police Station with Jorge Manuel and don Fernando.

Jorge Manuel and don Fernando were seated at the same conference table that they had sat at a few weeks earlier for their meeting with Mr. Jones. Don Fernando had told his nephew not to worry, that he would handle these new visitors.

Glenn Richardson, Dr. Carlson, and the entourage of attorneys filed in. Introductions were made. When everyone was seated, Glenn Richardson started to speak. "Gentlemen, the reason for today's meeting is..."

But don Fernando interrupted him. "We know why you are here, señor. You want your clinic back. That is no problem. We are done with our investigation. We have removed the guards and the police tape from the clinic. Here are your keys to the building. We have previously returned all the patient records and accounting files to the late señor Jones. The only thing we are keeping are the illegal drugs that we seized during our raid. I'm sure you do not want them."

Don Fernando placed a large ring of keys on the conference table in front of Glenn Richardson.

One of the lawyers spoke up. "And our licenses and permits?"

"All reinstated," said don Fernando as he slid a manila envelope across the table. "You can open the clinic tomorrow morning and be back in business."

Glenn Richardson looked at the lawyers on his left and on his right. This was too easy. Was he working with a bunch of imbeciles? Why did he have to come all the way to Panama just to be handed some keys? Someone was going to answer for this. But all he said was, "Thank you." He picked up the keys and the manila envelope. He looked at the lawyers again. Evidently, there were no more questions. So, he stood up. Everyone on his side of the table also stood up, and they awkwardly left the room.

Outside of the police station, Glenn Richardson exploded at the lawyers. "What the fuck was that!? You told me that they were refusing to open the clinic!"

"That's what they've been telling us," said the boldest of the lawyers.

"I came all the fucking way down her to pick up some keys!!? You'd better get this clinic up and running today! I want progress reports every day from now on! Fucking idiots!"

And with that, Glenn Richardson climbed into the private car and told the driver to take him to the airport, leaving Dr. Carlson, the three lawyers, and the ex-assistant to the late Mr. Jones just standing there on the sidewalk, wondering if they still had jobs.

Back in the conference room, Jorge Manuel and don Fernando could hear Glenn Richardson yelling. There was a knowing smile on don Fernando's face.

"Well, Koki," don Fernando finally said, "what do you think?"

"I think they were surprised, uncle. I have to admit, I was a little surprised myself."

Don Fernando shrugged. "The writing was on the wall, Koki. I had a long talk with Dani yesterday, and he convinced me that eventually these gringos would succeed in opening the clinic. I tried everything I could to keep the clinic closed, but these people have so much money. They have paid off all the *diputados* in Panama City. Even Andrés Cordela can't resist them. It's very difficult to fight evil when evil is rich."

"At least they will rehire the nurses and other staff," said Jorge Manuel.

"Yes, Koki. There is that, and that is a good thing. You will have to prepare for many more gringos to come to La Chorrera. Maybe the city council will give you a budget to hire more police. You will need them."

CHAPTER TWENTY-THREE

Time is like a river. Sometimes it narrows and speeds up; other times it broadens and runs slow and deep. But in all cases, it never stops flowing past the little events in our lives that we think are so important. Thus it was that time flowed past in the little city of La Chorrera, and at the Crown Weight-Loss Clinic. The days became weeks. The clinic reopened and was soon crammed with fat tourists, eager to reshape what time and habit had done to their bodies. The stores and souvenir shops in La Chorrera welcomed the tourists back with open arms and open cash registers. The city council of La Chorrera was glad for the new tax revenue and even increased Jorge Manuel's budget. The judges in Panama City were glad not to have the *diputados* breathing down their necks. The *diputados* in Panama's legislature patted themselves on the back for bringing US investment to Panama as they laundered the cash they had received under the table. Wall Street embraced the rebranded Crown Weight-Loss Alliance IPO, conveniently forgetting about the drug-substitution scandal. J.P. Morgan watched the IPO stock soar, and then sold all their shares, making millions in the process. Everyone benefited. Everyone was happy... everyone except for don Fernando. Each day that went by troubled him more. He wasn't sleeping well. The officers at work noticed his dour disposition. He was irritable with people. His ability to concentrate suffered.

And one day, when he just couldn't stand it anymore, don Fernando called Dan and asked him to come by the police station late that afternoon. Dan was glad to hear from his old friend, and so he went down to the station. When he got there, don Fernando suggested they go for a walk.

The sun was just starting to go down and the afternoon was starting to cool off.

Since the Villa Rosario police station is located just a block from the town's Parque Central, the two men naturally walked in that direction. The Parque Central takes up an entire city block, with its tall mango and palm trees that shade the winding walkways and cement park benches. Don Fernando sat down on one of the benches and gestured for Dan to do the same.

"Something's been bothering me, mi amigo," don Fernando said. "But I don't know who to talk to about it. I thought... maybe I could talk to you."

"Of course," Dan said.

Don Fernando sat quiet for a moment, then started in. "You know, I have dedicated my entire life to fighting crime, to protecting my little town... And I've always thought it was just bad *people* that I was fighting... I don't know if I'm saying this right, but I would always divide people into one of two groups: there were good people, and there were bad people. Now, I know that everyone is a mixture. I understand that... in the middle, everyone is a mixture. But when you go to the extreme end of the bad side, there were always bad people I could point to and say, 'This one is not a mixture. This one is just a bad person.' Do you know what I mean, Dani?"

Dan nodded and said, "Yes, yes, I do. I've met many such people."

"Well, always in the past, when such a person came to my town and did evil things, I could always stop them. I could arrest them, or I could pick them up in the middle of the night and take them out to the woods and have a little chat with them And they would go away, Dani. They would go to jail, or move to Panama City or somewhere else, or just disappear. And then the evil thing they were doing would be stopped... How can I explain this? That when I stopped the *person*, I would be stopping the evil activity. They would be gone, and whatever evil they were doing would also disappear."

Don Fernando paused to gather his thoughts and then spoke again.

"Remember Matzel Davis, that gold dealer here in town a few years ago? Remember how he killed those Colombianos who were robbing his suppliers? I *knew* he had killed them. But I never arrested him. I never even talked to him about it. Why? Because those Colombianos were bad people. They were robbing and killing innocent miners, who were just trying to make a living panning for gold. When Matzel killed the Colombianos, the robberies stopped. Why should I arrest him? He had done the right thing. He had stopped evil. So, I let it go.

"And remember that poor deaf-mute boy, that got murdered in the bathhouse about ten years ago? The man that murdered him was a serial killer. When the parents of that poor boy decided to kill their son's murderer, I didn't stop them. To me, that was their right as parents. Hell, I even let them use my gun... When cancer attacks the body, you have to take the cancer out, in order to save the body. That's what I've always believed!"

Dan nodded as don Fernando talked. Dan wasn't sure where this was all leading, but clearly don Fernando was distraught, and had something to get off his chest, so Dan just let him talk.

"You know who taught me that, Dani? Father Lopez. He always said, 'when cancer attacks the body, you have to take the cancer out.' I really miss him, Dani. I trusted him. I *believed* him. But now... now, I am not so sure he was right. Maybe I don't understand evil. Or maybe there is a new kind of evil in the world. Maybe we are entering the end of days that the Bible warned us about, I don't know. But this new kind of evil seems bigger... it is like that story about the monster, where you cut off one head and two more grow back... I thought that Dr. Crown was evil for starting his clinic in La Chorrera, and then giving poison to all the people who trusted him. I think he killed that woman—I don't even remember her name now... Laura something—

but he killed her. And I think I killed other people, too. He could have killed *me* with his amphetamine! He was an evil man... I was not sorry when he was dead. But I thought, when he was gone, the clinic would disappear. I was wrong, Dani. Because then that Mr. Jones showed up, with lawyers, and all their money... And they bribed the *diputados*. And the *diputados* called the judges, and the judges called the city council of La Chorrera, and the city council started calling Koki... They would have fired Koki if the clinic didn't reopen. But I still was hopeful that it was possible to stamp out evil. And so... I was glad when Mr. Jones died, because I thought that that would *end it*... But then we got the call that this Glenn Richardson was coming to town... and then I realized it would never end. The evil was so big, Dani, that they would just keep sending more and more people down to reopen that clinic... it would never stop. And for the first time in my life, I had to let evil win."

Don Fernando sat silent. Finally, Dan said quietly, "I think the evil you're talking about is capitalism, don Fernando. And that is something very difficult to fight against. Maybe impossible. I think you did the best that you could."

Don Fernando shook his head. "I don't think so, Dani. The problem is that I'm not sure what I *should* have done. The thing I did was only what I had always done in the past, but it did not work... You know, in the past, when I didn't know what to do, I would always go visit Father Lopez. And if I had done something wrong, he would forgive me, and tell me what right thing I should do... I miss him, Dani. Since he died, I have no one to confess my sins to. No one to advise me."

Dan nodded. Father Lopez had been the spiritual leader of Villa Rosario for decades. But his death five years ago had left a sort of void in the community. The young priests who had taken over his position in the Church were just too young to give advice on anything.

"Yeah, I miss him too, don Fernando."

The sun was starting to sink behind the distant mountains. The shadows in the park were long. The air was cool.

"Dani, you are the only friend I have left that I can confide in. And I want to tell you something. But you have to promise you will never tell anyone else."

Dan looked at don Fernando. *Here it comes*, he thought to himself. "I promise," he said.

"I killed Dr. Crown," don Fernando said quietly. "I shot him in the head and made it look like a suicide. I was angry with him for trying to poison me. I was angry with him for killing that girl. I thought he was an evil man. I thought he was putting his patients in danger. I thought I was doing the right thing. I didn't know how else to stop him. I thought if he was gone, the clinic would go away..."

Dan took a deep breath, but just nodded his head.

"But then that Mr. Jones showed up. Him and his money and his lawyers. He was evil, too. He was going to reopen the clinic. And then, *he* figured out that I had killed Dr. Crown... so I killed him. I stole his wallet to make it look like a robbery... I told myself I was doing the right thing again. That I was stopping evil..."

The sky was turning dark. An evening breeze rustled the palm branches high in the trees.

Dan searched for the right words to say. He had known don Fernando for such a long time; he shared don Fernando's outlook on life; he too believed that evil was real, and that certain men were so evil that they had to be stopped. Dan thought back over his own life. He too had done many things outside of the law. He wasn't sure what to do with don Fernando's confession. But he knew he was in no position to pass judgment against his friend.

"Do you think what I did was a sin, Dani?"

"I'm not sure, don Fernando. To be honest, I'm just not sure... but I know that Father Lopez would have forgiven you. He would have made you do penance—probably a big penance—but he would have forgiven you."

"I think what I did was wrong, Dani... I think it was a sin."

Dan had never found himself in this position before.

"If it helps, don Fernando... *I* forgive you," he said.

"Thank you, Dani."

The stars were beginning to shine above. The two men sat quietly on the park bench, each wrapped in his own thoughts.

EPILOGUE

The nature of evil is just as difficult to define as the nature of grace. Evil always seems to start with ignorance and greed, just as grace seems to have its origins in wisdom and kindness, but beyond that, both phenomena are difficult to talk about. The actions of men are not always predictable, and luck and unforeseen consequences play a tremendous part in how things turn out. One thing seems consistent: when evil wins, it always feels normal. And when goodness and grace win, it always feels like a miracle.

Through the IPO process, Crown Weight-Loss Incorporated was rebranded as the Crown Weight-Loss Alliance. The company experienced steady growth and successfully opened new clinics in Mexico, the Dominican Republic, and Aruba. They poured money and lobbyists into the thirty states that had laws against online medical services, and those states began to fall like dominoes. The Crown Weight-Loss Telehealth Program became *the* model for successful online distribution of semaglutide weight-loss drugs. The name Crown became as well-known as Walmart and Amazon. Millions of clients all over the United States were receiving their Ozempic, Wegovy, or Rybelsus medications via FedEx. The Crown Weight-Loss Alliance began to expand into Europe.

Back in La Chorrera, the Crown Weight-Loss Clinic became accepted as just part of the local economy. Jorge Manuel was kept busy with his growing city. Enrique Calvino returned to his job driving around the city of La Chorrera in his police car, and waving to the locals. Ana Luisa joined a Zumba class. Don Fernando started attending Mass every Sunday. And Dan fell back into his retired lifestyle in Villa Rosario.

And this is where our story ends, dear Reader. As with all real events in life, there can be no resolution. It simply rolls on, with or without you. When evil wins, it feels normal. When goodness wins, it feels like a miracle.

-fin-

ABOUT THE AUTHOR

Robert Rahula was born in Spain to an American father and Spanish mother but grew up in Virginia on the farm of his paternal grandparents. He returned to Menorca, Spain in the 1960s to pursue his writing career. Over the past thirty years, Robert has published dozens of books of prose and poetry in Spain and in the United States. Readings of his poems appear on his YouTube channel, his Facebook page, and his website robertrahula.com. He travels Europe and Central and South America for several months a year, giving readings and lectures, and spends the rest of his time writing.

9 798989 723812